Are There Sinners in Heaven?

Elizabeth Sorrells

Are There Sinners in Heaven?

ISBN: 978-1-7363658-3-0 (Paperback)

ISBN: 978-1-7363658-2-3 (eBook)

Library of Congress Control Number: 2021919757

Any references to historical and biblical events, real people, or real places are used fictitiously. Names, characters, and places are a product of the author's imagination.

Written by Elizabeth Sorrells

Cover image by ABIOLAGFX

Edited by M. Goodroad

First Published 2022

The Holy Bible: King James Version. Iowa Falls, IA: World Bible Publishers.

For Angie,
our guardian angel

Chapter 1

I spent years in what I call "the hole." Others just call it depression. It—and my anxiety—kept me from doing what I love, from *being* who I love. Life never seemed to let up.

At first, everything that affected me was big, like losing a job or family member. Something that would hurt anyone. Slowly, smaller and smaller things would upset me. Things like the battery in my remote dying would make me cry. I felt so lost and alone.

I knew I had people to support me, but it always felt as if I were a burden to them. So often, I just suffered alone. I let the bumps in the road become cliffs for me.

After a year or so, I began hallucinating, living in fear of what only I could see, of what voices lurked in the shadows of my mind. My only refuge was staying home with my dog, Milo. Milo was a great listener; he never judged me, never twisted my words. He just listened as I cried.

His white and black fur was soft between my fingers as I petted him. I would tell him everything, talking to him as though he would answer me.

I lived my days by counting tears, not blessings. I would stay up during the night, afraid of the dark things I saw moving in the corner or staring at me from beside my bedpost. The things from my childhood that went bump in the night still haunted me.

During the day, I would distance myself from my friends and family. It got to the point some of my friends assumed I was dead. It was like every day pealed another layer from my soul.

My memories began to taunt me. Memories of happiness and bright, joyful days were so distant, I felt as though I could never reach them again. The voices in my head never stopped. They were always whispering harsh lies to me.

I listened to every word like it would be the last voice I ever heard. *You don't belong here. No one will ever want you. There is no love for you.* It was painful to hear all day. I just dealt with it, taking in what I heard, and believing it. What kind of a life was that?

In my memories of my youth, I was one of only two Christians in a mainly atheist family. My grandfather was the rock that I built my faith upon. We were strong believers.

When my grandfather got sick, I had to walk myself to church. It was not very far, just far enough to make my feet tingle. In those days, when I was alone, I often thought of him. I never expected him to go so soon.

I went to a local church. It was not very big, but the faith in the room could be felt. Most of my friends went to that small church. Sunday school there was a miniature heaven for me. I enjoyed it—quite honestly, it was my favorite activity of the week.

As time passed and I got older, the shadows grew, and the voices got louder. My rock was gone, and I was left standing on tear-stained sand. I questioned my beliefs, and doubt crept in.

I fell in with the wrong crowd. I was sad and lonely then. I convinced myself there was no

God, no gracious Lord listening to a tiny speck like me. I told myself that He did not exist. The worst part was that I believed it.

I looked at the sky and stopped seeing heaven. I only saw the dark clouds. The sun was an annoying ball of light then, not a gift from a greater being. I ignored every miracle I witnessed.

Every day became a constant battle in my mind. Voices that started as soft whispers became consistent shouting day and night. They began to take over, stomping out my childish light. It became more difficult to block out every wrong thing they said. It was hard not to believe the voices in my head.

All the "don'ts" and "can'ts," all the "you don't matters" and "they don't cares" became my reality. My mind became my worst enemy. I never went to a doctor or even back to church to look for help. I let myself stay alone.

I found myself drifting into the dark, only ever letting specks of light in. It was like I was punishing myself but blaming God for it. Things felt like they would never look up, never get better in any way. So, I decided I would never feel this way again. I let the sun touch me one last time before the darkness crowded me like vultures. I took one last walk at dusk, just to watch the sun set.

It was a cool night in October. The stars were shining brightly, and in my mind, they were cheering me on. The moon cast shadows across my room as she shed star dust tears for me. All was calm. There was no sound except the cars passing on the street below.

I sat on my couch. The shadows from the moonlight haunted me. Whispers in my head began saying, *You don't belong here. No one will actually miss you. Just do it.* So, I did. I started by writing out a note. The pen left smooth ink behind on the page.

I found a few pill bottles, dumping them into my hands. I counted them one by one. In my hand was the mute for the voices. I silently prayed, one last time, for my peace. Then, I took them.

The pills stuck in my throat, water being my momentary savior. I laid back on the couch, my world slowly hazing out. It felt peaceful. A sudden barking snapped me back partially. A knock at the door sounded. I heard the door click open. I heard my name shouted out. I scowled. My closest friend had popped in for a surprise visit; such was my luck. I was annoyed. I wanted to die in peace with my note in hand.

"Lea, you'll be okay," I remember her vowing.

I am not sure what happened next. All I can remember is the sirens. They were like angels' voices. A gloved hand touched me.

"You'll be alright." The words sounded far away.

In that moment, I wanted to run back to my room and away from all the people who gathered around me. My friend's voice came again. Then, I wanted to run to her. If I were to die with someone near me, I did not want it to be the strangers loading me into the ambulance.

The heart monitor beeped desperately. I coughed some. The world slowly dimmed down to a dull grey, then everything went black. I felt like I was floating for a moment, like water surrounded me. It was wonderful. I felt a hand grab my shoulder and pull me close. The world felt warm.

Chapter 2

A harsh light blinded me as I opened my eyes. They stung as I squinted against it, blinking to adjust. As I blinked, a man appeared before me. I looked around, hoping that I was waking up in the hospital, alive and well. A twinge of regret for my actions bit at me. The only thing in sight was the man and pure white, though.

He had deep, forest green eyes that were shining brightly. He had a beard, short and brown, much like his hair. He smiled at me, a smile so friendly it was as if he had known me all my life. He reached out, took me by the hand, and helped me to stand.

I studied his features, looking for something. He was so familiar yet so new. Had I met this man before? Did I know his name? Or had he been from some forgotten dream?

"Where am I?" My words echoed along unseen walls, and my body seized, surprised by the booming.

My new companion laughed. His smile was my first comfort in that place.

"Somewhere you need to be, dear child," he said.

I looked around. There was nothing. It was like the inside of a cloud on a sunny spring day. I was afraid. Still, it was peaceful there. I looked back at the man. His white clothing hung loosely across him; his wings sparkled.

"Then who are you?" I glared at him, searching for some sign of fear I could play on. He still smiled that warm, loving smile.

"An angel. *Your* angel to be exact." His eyes softened.

As he stepped closer, I took a step back. This place was so confusing and new. I had no idea where I was. *Maybe heaven?* I looked around. There were no streets of gold, no shining cities. It was all just white. A pure, shining light that I had never seen before.

I turned back to the angel. "Why am I here? Why are you here?"

"*You* are here to learn," he chuckled, "*I* am just your guide."

He waved his arm. The solidness of the white changed

slowly, morphing into a familiar room. Light browns and heavy greens formed with an old, brown plaid couch. I felt tears in my eyes. I knew it in an instant; it was Paw's house. I looked around. Each old picture was in the right place, even the crooked picture of my grandma. A soft cough sounded behind me.

I turned quickly, and there he was. His old grey hairs were the same. The smile on his face was familiar, and his eyes shined with life. This was the man I remembered.

"Paw…" The word barely came.

The tears fell softly as I walked across the plush carpet. It still felt bouncy underfoot. I reached my hand out, not believing that I could touch him; I was afraid that he would disappear if I did. He grabbed my hand and nodded. I pulled him close into a hug. I stared at the wall as he held me. I had missed him.

I took a deep breath in to calm myself. Last time I had seen him was in a hospital bed, looking pale and thin. I quivered at the thought. My heart stopped and an ice pick went through it when I looked up to meet his eyes.

He looked at me, defeated. It was as though he were lost in the world. He opened his mouth, hesitating some.

"Lea sweet child," he shook his head, "what have you done?"

I looked away quickly, not meeting his eyes. He let out a heavy breath as he sat down; no bones creaked with aged efforts this time.

"I don't understand." He made me look him in the eye. "What could you have done to think this was right?"

I bit my lip nervously. He shook his head at me slowly. He sat me down on the couch, patting my knee. A sigh escaped his lips.

"I almost did the same thing, you know," he started. "I once was so lost I felt there was no other option. But I stayed strong. I wish you had, too."

"Paw, I'm not as good of a person as you are," I tried to reason with him.

"I wish that were true. Let me introduce you to someone," he motioned towards the shadows.

A young girl walked out of them. She had long black hair and beautiful dark brown eyes. She looked up at me with understanding eyes. They were softened by the dull glow of sadness.

"During the war, I was told to kill everyone that came into sight, and this child came out. I… I shot her. She was as innocent as a butterfly. I followed my orders well, I even received metals, but nothing could make me regret what I had done less." He let a single tear slide down his cheek. His eyes sparkled with tears.

"This is Hoa." Paw looked at her sadly. "I always hated myself for all the death I caused. But I know He forgives me, and so does Hoa." He smiled to the girl.

"Who is 'He'?" I asked softly.

"Jesus." Paw nodded, a soft grin gracing his tear-stained cheeks.

"Jesus doesn't exist. This is all some sort of dream," I snapped, pinching myself in an attempt to wake up.

I looked around, seeing the angel again. He stood near my grandfather. Paw stood slowly, taking Hoa's hand. Paw pulled the angel closer, whispering something to him.

I ignored it. I wanted to wake up. I wanted to open my eyes and be home in my bed. Paw walked past me and patted me on the back.

"You'll figure it out. Just trust your angel." He walked away and out of the front door, pausing in the door frame. He looked back at me with tear-heavy eyes.

"I love you," I yelled to him as he passed through the door. He paused again to smile at me before shutting the door. I stared at the door for a moment, sniffling as I felt my nose grow warm and the tears form in my eyes.

I turned to the angel, who stared at me for a second. I gave him a sad-eyed look, hoping he would take pity on me and send me home. He laughed and shook his head.

"No, dear child. It is not time to go home. You have many more to meet."

Meet? I thought to myself, *I don't even want to be here. Now I have to meet new people?*

Angel chuckled as though he had heard my thoughts.

"Go out the back door." He pointed. His white robe waved with the motion.

I walked towards the door, opening it slowly. It still creaked the way it always had.

"Jeremiah will not be alone here," he said when he noticed me looking back desperately.

Jeremiah was Paw's real name. I felt shivers as I opened the door all the way. The white room opened again. It was blindingly bright, just as it had been before. I blinked my eyes hard, trying to adjust them.

"It will get better soon," Angel said.

I walked on. There was nothing there but the blinding pureness. There were walls. I could not see them, but words often echoed off them. I paused for a moment. I wanted to go home where there was no harsh light or angels. Then, I thought harder. Was life on Earth really better? I remembered all the pain I had gone through there.

I shivered. I was not sure what I wanted to do. There, wherever I was, felt safe. Earth did not. At the same time, I knew I had family on Earth and Milo.

My heart dropped; I had just left Milo. I stood still for a moment until I felt Angel's wing brush against my back, gently pushing me forward.

"You will meet a new Jeremiah." Angel's words sounded far away.

I heard a soft cry in the distance. Then the door shut behind me. I looked back; Angel trailed behind me as we walked.

In those few seconds between what could only be described as rooms, I felt alone. That is until a hand touched my shoulder. It startled me, stopping me on the path. I shivered. Soon, a calm drifted over me, like warm sunlight on a cool fall day.

I felt cold once the hand was gone. But I shook the feeling off, looking forward in the harsh, snowy light.

Chapter 3

I felt a weight on my arm. It shifted some. I looked down, and there, in my arms, was a small infant. He opened his crystal blue eyes and blinked at me.

"Jeremiah?" I turned to Angel in question.

He nodded with a soft grin. The baby cooed to me, giggling softly. A crashing wave of warmth splashed over me. The warmth was soothing and left me feeling at home and happy. I looked at the child, just to feel the same wave again. This feeling was completely foreign to me.

"Angel, what is this feeling?" I asked without looking up.

"A familial love. A mother's love," he chuckled.

A mother's love, I repeated in my mind. A deep passion filled me along with a strong need to protect the small child. It was wonderful. My Jeremiah turned towards me and drifted into a momentary, docile sleep. I watched him. His soft snores melted me.

As I watched him sleep, I saw our future together. He changed from baby to toddler until he was, I guessed, about fourteen. I saw bumps and bruises, casts and crutches, loose teeth and happy smiles.

He stopped and looked at me. His beautiful, short red hair was ruffled; he looked like me. I melted when he smiled at me. Pulling me close, he hugged me tightly. His skin had no temperature, but I closed my eyes. I took a deep breath in. The scent of tulips tickled my nose.

"Mama," he grinned. "You look so beautiful!"

I could not respond, the words stopped in my throat. I looked him up and down. *This is definitely a dream.* I shook my head. There was no way I was meeting my unborn son, no way there was an angel guiding me through it.

I was not in love; I was not even sure if I was alive. Jeremiah could not be my child. I did not want to be a mother only because I knew I would be horrible at it. I stepped back some.

Jeremiah looked at me sadly. Fear and disappointment tainted his once sweet gaze.

I met his eyes for a moment.

"I-if you are here…" His words trailed off into silence. "I don't want to choose another mother," he sobbed, holding me around my waist tightly. "I chose you myself. You're the one I want. Only you!"

His tears were cold; one of the only temperatures in that world. I heard soft whispers in the back of my head: *Worthless. Heartless. Selfish.* My mind repeated what Jeremiah had said, twisting his words into painful knifes in my heart. His cries became words of hatred in my mind.

My heart was torn in two. I wanted to live for him now, but I was still unsure if I wanted to live for myself. I felt a stab inside me. Jeremiah had picked me.

That meant he saw something I did not. He saw some good in me. I felt warm again, knowing I had to live for him, to live up to his expectations. I did not know how much time it would take to be a good enough person for such a perfect child. I wanted to go home.

"There has to be a way. I want to go home, Angel," I urged him as I looked around for a door.

"There is still time, dear child. First, there are more to meet." He smiled. "Jeremiah will be waiting for you."

I turned to Jeremiah with a sigh. He was still heartbroken. I had to hurry; I knew in my heart I needed to get out of there. I moved his red hair from his forehead, kissing it softly.

"I want to go back. I want to live for you. I want to be there for you. I want to give you the best life Earth has to offer." I held him tightly as I spoke.

"Thank you, Mama. Stay safe, and remember God loves you."

He smiled softly, sniffling as he dragged his arm across his nose.

I smiled uncomfortably but kissed his head again. *Anything for him,* I told myself with confidence. I saw Jeremiah filter into a soft, pale glow. The blue orb floated off into the distance. I looked at it sadly.

"Where is he going?" I asked Angel without turning to him.

"Back to heaven to wait for you." He nodded, touching my shoulder.

He turned me slowly to the right, pointing to a door

beginning to form. The silver handle turned itself.

"Who will I meet next?" I blinked in the light.

There was a short walk, a little further than I'd walked before meeting my Jeremiah. As we moved slowly, the room formed into a cooled winter street.

"You may not know him," Angel said.

"Another child of mine?" I asked with a sharp, excited heartbeat jumping through me.

He shook his head slowly, sighing lightly. "This man has

watched over you since a week after he met you."

I nodded, slightly confused. Angel seemed calm, not looking down at me. I trusted him. I let my mind wander to who this man could be. *This is so strange,* I thought to myself. *Angels, dead family members, and an unborn child. What next?* I heard Angel snicker a little. I smiled to him.

He held out his arm, letting me pass. I walked by, looking for the next person. Bushes began to line up down an invisible road. Houses mapped out a hidden city.

I bounced slightly, excited to meet the next person. The world fell into the full street of my childhood on a Sunday afternoon after a long rain. Thin sheets of ice layered against the street. The scent of the Earth was tart. I remembered that day.

Chapter 4

A small, red-headed girl walked into view from down the street. Each step was slow and deliberate. She slipped on a small ice patch but caught herself. She giggled lightly as she slid down the hill.

I laughed to myself, smiling at her joy. Her thick boots swallowed her small feet and thin legs. A puffy jacket kept her warm; the iridescent pink exterior was battered and ripped. The child was loudly singing Sunday School songs she had learned.

I turned to Angel; his eyes softened as he looked at the child. I turned back to her. We watched as she stopped to play in the snow.

I watched as a car pulled up behind her. The driver's smile was kind, but his eyes held a deep, wily look. He stopped beside her and began talking.

"Hello, little one." He smiled. "Can you help me find the hospital?"

I glared at him, I remembered that day well. It was

Sunday and in Sunday School we learned about the good Samaritan and I saw no one else to help the man. I agreed quickly, eager to be that kind person from the story.

"Hop in my car. You can tell me how to get there. I have a bad memory," he grinned.

As I opened the door, police sirens sounded, though the cause of the noise was not obvious. The man rushed off, leaving my younger self behind. He hit black ice, spinning out of control and hitting a pole.

Younger me ran to our grandfather, telling him of what happened. The snow landed on our eyelashes as she ran as fast as she could. Paw opened the door and held her. I shook some, now knowing the weight of the situation. I could have been kidnapped.

I felt a hand touch my shoulder. I turned, and there stood the man. His eyes were filled with sorrow. He looked at me for a long moment. He did not speak at first, just stared at me.

"I…I am so sorry," the man started.

"You should be," I snapped. "Who knows what you could've done. I was just a kid. I thought I would be helpful, but I could've been hurt, sold, or even killed."

"Please, hear me out, Lea," the man begged.

"I don't see why I should." I spoke through gritted teeth.

"Child, please. Listen." Angel tried to reason with me.

I nodded in response. I looked the man up and down. His clothes were baggy and worn. His hair was dirty, and his skin was rough.

He took a ragged breath in, his eyes wavered as though he were rethinking meeting me.

Now, he regrets it? I scoffed in my mind.

"You see," the man gulped, "I was a self-medicator. I used anything to hide the pain of losing my daughter to social services. The loss of her mother was the hardest thing I've lived through."

I looked down at my feet. I did not want to hear his sad story. This man was evil. I did not think he belonged wherever we were, he did not deserve to meet me.

He continued, "She died of cancer, and after that, I was a horrible father. I focused on my own pain. I drank until I couldn't even take my baby to school. After she was taken away, I… I just started doing worse. I would've used you to get more things to fuel my addictions.

"I kept using drugs to help me feel physically better after the wreck you saw me in. It then hit me how badly I was behaving. I went to church one Sunday, and I prayed in a way I never had before. I begged for forgiveness; I tried to change. I stopped all the drugs. Really, I tried to stop it all. But I kept drinking until one day when I never woke up from a drunken nap. I have tried to watch over you and my daughter since."

I stared at him. Silence filled the street. The man hung his head. I heard him start sobbing before he collapsed to the ground. It felt like there was a fire in my soul, a fire fueled by hatred.

I looked down at him. *Pitiful,* I thought to myself. *He is pitiful.* I felt a tap on my arm. Angel had batted at me with his wing. I sighed aloud, patting the man on the back.

"Lea, please forgive me. I know my daughter may never, but please. I need someone to forgive me for the horrid life I lived," he begged.

"Why don't you ask Jesus? Everyone here seems to think that's the fix to all the world's problems." I rolled my eyes.

Angel and the man both flinched at my words. The man sighed heavily, and Angel shook his head.

"Lea, listen to Gabriel. He is regretful. He just asks for forgiveness." Angel spoke, motioning to the man.

"Gabriel," I turned to the man, "I can't forgive you. Not today. I am a bitter person. Use your 'God' for forgiveness, not me."

Angel grabbed my hand as I turned to walk away. He gave me a harsh glance. I had not seen Angel upset like that in the time I had known him.

"Fine," I growled. "I forgive you."

"It has to be genuine, Lea." Gabriel looked at me with heavy, sad eyes.

I sat on the ground with a huff. I did not want to forgive this man. He seemed retched, even after hearing his story. I grumbled angrily to myself. *This is stupid! Why should I forgive him?*

"You do not have to forgive him today. You just need to learn to move past your anger." Angel nodded to the man as he walked slowly away.

"And why should I?" I snapped.

"Lea, this man has watched over you since the day he died. He spent more than half your life protecting you from many harms," Angel reasoned.

"Yeah? Like him?" I smirked in triumph as Angel let out a heavy sigh. He fluttered his wings in frustration.

"You are here to learn to let go of earthly pettiness. A true Christian would forgive in time," Angel argued on Gabriel's behave.

"Well, maybe I'm not a 'true Christian,'" I snapped aloud.

"You will be in time." Angel walked to me, wrapping his wing around me. "For now, just say what you are feeling."

"I feel upset. Something bad could've happened to me, because of *this* man. I'm being asked to forgive him, and that's making me mad," I spoke with a harsh tone.

"You know, Jesus has forgiven many people who have done Him wrong." Angel spoke without looking at me. He started alone towards Gabriel.

"I'm not Jesus." I stared hard at Angel's back.

"I never said you were. I am just saying to live as He would." Angel smiled softly.

Gabriel turned as we came closer. His smile was kind. He seemed much happier and at peace. He turned to me and sighed.

"Lea, I understand you may not want to forgive me, but—" he started.

"I can try to forgive you, Gabriel. It may take me a while, but I can try, right?"

I faked a smile. The fire in me dulled, though I still did not like the man. I looked around me.

Angel smiled. He knew I was not being completely honest, but part of me believed maybe I could.

Gabriel kissed my hand softly. His eyes shone with tears. He tried to speak, but his words were broken.

"Y-you tru-truly are a-a good Christian, Lea." He smiled as he stood and walked us to the door. He opened it for Angel and me.

I walked through the doorway completely, and once I did, the walk once again lengthened. I looked around; nothing was there but the same purity. As we reached the next space, the world became calm; an antique feeling came over me. A woman stood before me. I knew her.

Chapter 5

The room was older than Paw's, a soft cream color painted on the walls. Sunlight filtered in through white lace curtains. Picture frames hung on the wall, faces smiling in each one. A sweet, old perfume tickled my nose.

My great grandmother stood before me in the center of the room, her smile as beautiful as it had always been. Her hair was put up in a tall beehive, and it was a beautiful grey. Her hair complimented her kind face.

She walked up to me slowly and placed her hands on my cheeks. She wiped a tear away as it slid down my face. I hated not feeling the warmth of her touch. It hurt knowing she was there, yet all I could feel was a pressure against me. It made me feel alone. Then I met her eyes.

Her eyes—her beautiful eyes—were as gentle as they had been in life. I stared into them. They welcomed me with a loving gaze.

"You look just like your mother."
She let a faint smile be painted
across her face.

I placed my hands on hers,
feeling the texture of her skin. It
felt the same as it always had, the
way I remembered it.

"I'm so glad to see you here,
MiMi," I whimpered.

I let more tears come. She
had passed when I was young,
but I was still lucky enough to
remember having precious days
with her. I lived in the memories
of us making things and baking
sweets together.

I remembered her cookies and the perfect aroma of the baked goods mixed with her old perfume. I had loved those flour-covered days we spent together.

Those memories I cherished drifted away. My new reality took hold of me as MiMi kissed my cheek softly then pulled away from me quickly.

"Child," she sighed, "why on God's green Earth would you try and take your own life?"

Her words were clouded with grief and anger. I looked down at my feet, scared to meet her eyes. I had begun to realize the real reason why.

"I thought I was a mistake, MiMi…" My words trailed away. I felt my eyes stinging, as I sniffled loudly.

"Now, the good Lord makes no mistakes. You learned that in Sunday School, and we both know it."

I looked up at her, shocked. She had passed the day before I had learned that lesson. I remembered it well because I refused to believe it. Why would He take someone else from my life? She and Angel looked at each other. She smiled a little and shook her head.

"You seemed to have forgotten a lot. You used to tell me my father watched me from heaven, even though you had never met him. And when I first passed, you knew I was watching you." She shook her finger at me.

I looked down. I could not meet her eyes. I knew the ocean blue eyes could see right through me. She always had a way of knowing what was wrong in my life. She pulled me close and started stroking my hair. Her fingers tangled in it more than once. She kissed my head repeatedly, each kiss ending with a loud smack.

I took in deep, steady breaths. "I was all alone, MiMi," I finally cried aloud.

"You were never alone, child." A hand touched my back. "All of us were here."

Paw was behind me, his hand the one I felt against my back. His eyes were soft as he looked at me.

All of us? I questioned in my mind. A door began to appear before me. I shivered. *All of us?*

Angel walked me towards it.

I stopped at the door, seeing my reflection in the

handle. *All of us?* Was I really ready to meet who I thought was behind the door?

I backed away a bit. I was *not* ready to meet her. I never would be. I walked further away from it.

Angel stepped in front of me and tried to usher me toward the door. I shook my head angrily, pushing against him.

"Angel, I don't want to." My voice cracked.

Paw and MiMi looked at me with sad eyes then back to the door as though silently praying I would walk through it and face the giant fear in my heart.

Angel held my hand and began leading me back to the door. I pulled my hand away and ran. I ran from the room I was in out into the light.

"Lea…" I heard Angel's voice in the distance.

I ran faster. I was not ready to move to the next room. I did not know if I wanted to see her. So much fear and anger filled me.

My legs began to hurt as I kept running. I slowed, my breathing heavy. I looked around;

nothing was there but the shining purity that surrounded me.

It was strange to me that my angel could morph the light into worlds. The snow-like appearance of the place startled me. I felt the empty space closing in on me.

I began shaking, my body quivering as I stood. Darkness edged my vision, and my eyes stung with how widely I held them open. My legs felt heavy. Then I fell to my knees.

Tears raced down my cheeks. They were freezing, and in a temperature-less world, it was welcomed. My stomach twisted in a painful way. I leaned over, my hair falling around my face as I cried in a scream.

My heart beat faster than it ever had, like it was trying to pound its way out of my chest; my breath caught in my throat. *All of us.* The words came again.

"Please, Lea. This may help you." Angel appeared beside me.

"No, Angel. I can't. I can't," I sobbed aloud.

His eyes were shattered with sadness. He helped me to my feet, letting me cry on his white-robed shoulder.

He walked me towards the door. The distance seemed much greater as we walked slowly together.

I sniffled as we continued. "Why her?" I cried again.

"Dear child, you have imagined this moment throughout your entire life. I am sorry it brings you such pain, but it is something you need to do to continue on our journey," Angel explained softly.

The door was there, in the distance, it's handle showing my reflection once more as I grew closer. I shivered again.

Angel opened the door slowly. I stumbled through it, drying a few of my own tears. The world flashed in my eyes before Angel changed the light into a small nursery. Pastel pinks shined in the natural, pale light from an open window.

Chapter 6

I looked down at my feet as we walked towards the center of the room. I refused to look up, but I saw the tips of her shoes. I took a breath in until my lungs felt completely stretched out, like they were going to burst. I let it out in a big sigh.

I looked up, and there was a beautiful woman standing before me. Her blue eyes softly gazed at me. Her lips were stretched into a beautiful smile.

Her curly red hair reached the middle of her back.

"Lea, honey, why are you here so soon?" she asked in a whimper.

"What do you care?" I responded coldly.

She flinched at my words but never lost that sweet smile. Shifting her weight onto one leg, she stood in silence, looking for the right words.

"It wasn't my choice," she whispered.

"How was it not your choice?" I snapped. "Why didn't you just fight harder or tell God to wait?

Anything to have stayed with me."

Her eyes shone with years of pain. She just shook her head, a single tear slipping down her thin face.

"Baby, it wasn't my choice," she sighed.

I turned away from her, walking to the corner of the nursery. I looked down at my crib, my favorite stuffed animal laid beside the small, folded blanket.

"It *was* your choice." I barely voiced the words.

"Sometimes, we can't control our lives," she explained to me.

"Yeah. I know," I started. "All the bullying from only having a father. I was too 'tomboy' to play with the other girls at recess. I was raised by a widowed father, and his job wasn't great. So, we struggled for years. I had to play 'mom' just because our family didn't have one."

I felt Angel's hand on my shoulder. I looked back at him. He glanced straight at my mother, and I turned to watch her. She was sobbing on her knees.

She looked up at me, the whites of her eyes stained red.

Sniffling, she slowly stood and walked over to me.

"Lea—" she started.

"No," I interrupted her. "I don't want your excuses. I don't want to hear what you have to say. You left us."

"I never left you. Just like your MiMi, I watched over you. I never left you, baby. I just wasn't there physically." My mother struggled to find the right words.

I plugged my ears and turned around. I was not going to listen to her lies. I looked around, desperate to find a door to escape through, but the only one I noticed was behind her.

I looked at Angel with pleading eyes, yet he shook his head at me. I knew it meant I had to face her and try to understand her side.

"But I don't want to, Angel," I begged.

"Lea, I cannot force you to stay and listen. All I ask is that you treat this as the first and last time with your mother," Angel explained.

The last time I see her? I asked myself. Then I remembered; there was a chance for me to go back to Earth. There was a chance to live my life, but this was my first and last impression.

"Lea, I was very sick when I was pregnant with you. I couldn't control what was happening. Sometimes, you just can't control life the way you want to." She walked closer to me then took my hand.

I pulled my hand away. I was not ready to listen to her. If she had really loved us, she would have lived for us. My father was lost without her; *I* was lost without her.

I looked around the room, taking in everything. The walls

were painted the way they had been when I was a kid. My mother walked beside me as I stared at the hand-done butterflies and ladybugs.

"We painted this room for you, your father and me. I was so excited to have a second baby girl." She dried one side of her face with her hand.

"Dad always told me it was your idea to paint the room lilac. I always loved that color." I sniffled as I placed my hand on the wall.

"I missed being there for you. I wanted to live for you." She tried to reason with me.

"My favorite memories are of sitting in Dad's lap and listening to the story of how he first met you." I felt tears forming in my eyes as I spoke distractedly. "He always told me he believed in angels only because he saw their beauty in you."

"I remember when I first saw him. He spilt his drink in his lap as he stared at me." She laughed fondly at the memory. "His smile is something I will never forget."

I sat in the rocking chair in the corner of my nursery. Its white paint was fading and chipping. I rocked in it for a while as I looked to my mother.

"I used to always imagine you in this rocking chair. We kept it in the office after we took it out of my nursery. It was almost like a real memory." I smiled, remembering.

"This was my mother's rocking chair. She gave it to me when she learned I was pregnant with your sister." Mom smiled.

"Growing up, I had so many questions for you." I sniffled softly.

"I wish I could have been there to answer them all." Mom kissed my forehead softly.

"Why was I so angry at you?" I asked as I began to cry harder.

"Because you just wanted my love, but you didn't know you've always had it." She rocked the chair gently.

"You've always loved me?" I looked up at her with sad eyes.

"Of course, my love. Ever since the second I knew you were growing inside me." She held my hand tightly.

I nodded as I held her hand. This was what I'd always wanted, to just hold my mother close. She walked to stand in front of me, helping me to stand.

"You know, the Lord is the same. He's loved you since before you came to Earth." She smiled.

"I'm not sure if I believe that." I shook my head.

"You will in time." She kissed my forehead and walked me to the door.

Angel stood next to it, opening it for me. As I began to walk through, I paused and ran back to my mother. I hugged her tightly.

"I love you," I whispered in her ear.

"And I will always love you." She kissed my cheek quickly.

I left that room and my mother, all just to begin a new section of my journey. I stepped into the light, and so it began.

Chapter 7

The white around me morphed into the familiar form of trees. Large oaks surrounded me. Birch and cherry trees were scattered throughout the trunks. Flowers tickled me as I walked by rose bushes that had grown as tall as me.

"Angel, where are we?"

He laughed with joy. "We are in the world designed by a once lost woman." His words confused me.

A woman trotted towards me from between the trees. She had beautiful mahogany skin, shining in the light. Her eyes held the look of a loving mother, like the eyes of *my* mother.

"Beautiful in every way." Her words came smoothly.

"No, I—"

She hushed me, taking my hand. She traced the scars on my arms, taking a short moment to kiss each one.

I stared in awe; true beauty stood before me. Her smile outshone the sun, her eyes more beautiful than the forest garden we stood in.

We walked together towards a large willow then sat under it on a log. She grinned still, her smile never wavering. I couldn't help but stare.

"Dear, sweet Lea…" She finally spoke again. Her words were like the sweet birds' songs that surrounded us. "You think you are but a mistake?"

"I- I—Yes."

"Oh, child, you are no more a mistake than I am. And I was the first woman." She laughed aloud.

"Eve?" I gasped loudly.

"Ah, a smart one!" She turned and winked at Angel.

She stood and waltzed around me, stopping to braid my hair with flowers.

I sat in silence, listening to her hum different songs, none that I knew yet somehow still familiar. I took a deep breath, relishing the sweet scents of the beautiful garden. "Eve?" I finally spoke.

She looked at me. "Yes, little one?"

"Why did you do it?" I asked softly, wanting to hear her talk more.

"I was wondering when you would ask that," she chuckled.

"I-I'm sorry. I was just curious."

"Oh, no, my dear. I do not mind the question. I have answered it more times than I can count." Her smile softened.

Eve walked in front of me, sitting softly in the grass. Angel shuffled over and sat under a tree in the distance. She looked out into the horizon as though to remember her youth.

"The serpent tempted me," she sighed, "and like every human since, I sinned. Maybe it was destined to happen; maybe it was just a young mistake. One way or another, the past will remain in the past. There is no reliving life. You can only move forward."

I nodded, taking her words deeply into my mind. I looked at her again, trying to memorize her features before the door appeared once more. Her hair was long and black. Her eyes still shone in a gentle gaze.

She looked down and away from me. Words seemed to be locked in her throat.

"Just remember: live your life the best way possible; if not for yourself, for someone else." She smiled sadly.

"But I don't have anyone to live for. I live alone," I tried to argue.

"You have people in heaven to live for, just as you do on Earth. Your friends, your family, even Milo." She chuckled.

My heart dropped at Milo's name. I hadn't thought of him much since I'd awakened in that world. Had someone been taking care of him, feeding and walking him? Or was he all alone, sad and scared? I began to wonder exactly how long I had been gone.

I turned back to Eve, Milo still fresh in my mind. "What do

I do when I get back to Earth? Will everything be the same?"

"That is something you must figure out on your own." She held my hands.

Her eyes drifted back to my arm. She traced the scars lightly, memories in her eyes as she began to talk.

"My Cain had a scar. A demon of jealousy caused him to kill his brother, and God gave him a mark to remind him of what he'd done. Cain had to face his demons alone from then on. How many demons have you faced while getting yours?" Her eyes were sad as she met mine.

I shivered uncomfortably, choosing to ignore her question. I looked back, desperate to see my Angel.

A door appeared in a tree, a bronze handle with it. Angel stood and walked me towards it. He turned the knob slowly, opening the door without a word.

I looked back to see Eve. Adam was with her now, kissing her gently. Their white robes intertwined. Pale wings seemed to appear from their backs. They were beautiful. I smiled as we walked through the door together.

The light reappeared. I found a comfort in it now. I shivered as we paced down a new, shining path, paved with gold. It was as beautiful as I had imagined heaven to be.

We walked down the path in silence. It was a perfect, shining world. I loved it, yet something about it felt secluded and lonely.

I took a deep breath in, relishing the calm hum of the world, sung like the hymns of my childhood. Soon, we found ourselves in the usual white room.

My angel swiped his arm, introducing a new world. I watched in amazement as it swirled into existence. It was lovely. I looked around the room, excited to see what formed next, desperate to meet more people.

Chapter 8

A small house formed in the distance, a dirt path connecting it to where we stood. A woman with dark hair stood in the doorway. Her deep brown eyes were bright and happy. She walked quickly away from the house before meeting me and pulling me into a hug.

"Perfect. Absolutely perfect," she breathed as she looked me up and down.

"No." I shook my head and looked down.

"Hush, child." The woman grabbed my hand and walked with me. I stayed nervously beside her. She looked down to watch our feet as we went, and she seemed lost in memories.

When she finally looked up at me, I saw older days dancing through her shining eyes. I glanced over my shoulder at Angel, who trailed behind us. He looked around as we walked back down the dirt path.

The woman had loose cloths hanging from her arms. Holding my hand tighter, she led me into the house and sat me down at the table near the back of the house.

I looked around the small place. A glassless window was on one wall next to the doorway. We sat down at the table.

A small wooden table sat to the side of the room, near the window. An open fire was in the middle of the room, I watched as it flickered.

Pulling my attention back to the woman, she invited me to sit on the blankets next to the table. I noticed a pitcher and two cups.

"You know," she did not meet my eyes as she poured water into the two cups, "once, long ago, I was told I would birth a Savior for the world."

"Mary?" I asked her.

"That is my name, yes." Mary giggled to herself. She paused for a moment, setting the water vase down. She looked to Angel, and with the glance, he escorted himself out.

Mary gave me a cup and sipped from her own. I took a gulp of the water, not realizing that it would be cold going down my throat.

"I was terrified," she finally broke the silence.

"Why? Didn't everything turn out well?"

"My world was very unaccepting of an unmarried woman expecting a child. Joseph could have had me sent away. He even had the right to have me stoned." She exhaled heavily.

"But he didn't," I pointed out.

"No. He was a good man." Her eyes softened at the thought of him. "But he only believed after he met Gabriel, the angel sent to us by God."

"Didn't Gabriel meet you first?"

"Yes, and I was afraid. Once I understood what was happening, I was overjoyed until I remembered what rights Joseph had. I knew I could die, but Gabriel met Joseph and saved me," she explained.

"Did you ever see him again after that?" I shifted in my chair to be closer to her.

She looked out the window, staring at a man talking with Angel. He was slightly taller than Angel with rugged features. He looked at me and waved before turning back to the deep conversation.

"He was there when Jesus was born. He brought the 'wise men' as you say now. He brought the shepherds. He even brought the other angels to worship the newborn Savior.

"Later, Gabriel told Joseph and me to flee. We went to Egypt, which saved Jesus from being killed as a child. Then, we saw him once again when an angel told us it was safe to return." She smiled as she spoke, remembering the story.

"Why do you tell me this?"

"Because God was moving in my life as he is now in yours."

I looked around the room, annoyed. God was not "at work" in my life. He never proved he was there all the times that I had begged him to. *I don't believe this*, I snapped in my mind.

My angel must have heard as he appeared behind me. I felt his hand on my shoulder. Looking up at him, I saw his sad gaze.

"Thank you, Mary, but Lea does not believe." He met my eyes as he spoke. His voice held a deep disappointment that sent shivers down me.

"I understand." She nodded at him. "I will pray that, one day, she will."

A hand touched my shoulder as Angel walked to stand in front of me. "A mother's prayer will always do good," a new and comforting voice added. I looked back, but no one was there. I took a deep breath in, ready to move on.

Angel and I left the house to travel around the rest of the large room we were in. We walked to a tree in the distance.

It was a large and sturdy tree with a door adorning it. It was pure white with a shining handle. I reached out to it, turning it slowly. The door remained silent as it swung open.

Angel walked solemnly beside me. He had lost his usual smile. The light engulfed us before forming a golden path. I shivered. It was so cold, so empty. I missed jumping from room to room with no path in between.

I looked around, desperate to find something to break the solid color. The only things were the golden path, the door ahead of me, and Angel and me.

I broke the silence. "Angel, are there sinners in heaven? Like, really bad sinners?"

He flinched at my question but answered, "Ask again later, child."

We had reached the door and Angel turned the handle, letting me into the next room. It began to form around me.

I looked at Angel one more time, desperate to see him looking happier. He did not look down to meet my eyes this time.

I sighed as we walked and began to notice the details of the new room. A large world seemed to spread out in front of me. It was beautiful.

Chapter 9

A small meadow sprouted around me. Tiny daisies budded, their white petals like snow against the green forest of grass. I smiled, plucking one to show my angel. Humming flooded the room. I turned to see a woman in a pastel-colored robe walking towards us. Her long hair blew gently in the wind. She walked to me, taking my hand.

She sat down and patted the vibrant grass beside her, so I

sat quickly, pulling my angel down with me. He huffed in protest but sat.

I waited for the woman to speak, looking into her sparkling eyes. She blinked slowly as the wind rustled our hair.

"Why do you think you are here, Lea?" she asked me.

"Because I died." I shrugged.

"No, dear girl. You are here to learn. You have given up hope when you should not have."

"What do you know about my life?" I snapped at her.

"No more than you know about mine." She grinned.

"I don't even know who you are!" I groaned in frustration.

She winked at Angel then stretched her legs out, laying back in the grass.

Dark clouds began to cover the shining sky. A soft rain drizzled down on us, cool on my scalp. I welcomed it.

Beside me Angel ruffled the feathers of his wings, mumbling to himself.

The woman laughed at him. "Tell me…" She turned to

me. "What is rain: good or bad? Happy or sad?"

"Well, it's good for the earth, but it makes me sad," I explained, half to her and half to myself.

"Learn to love the rain; learn not to see the darkness but the coming rainbow," she said as she rolled over in the grass.

I closed my eyes, turning my face to the rain. It was a momentary bliss, like the negativity of the world was being washed off me.

"Let Him find you in the rain. Let Him make you a rainbow. Know that He will if you trust Him."

Her words warmed me deep inside. Then, a dull light shone through my eyelids.

I shifted over then opened my eyes. I did not see the woman. I looked around desperately for her. "Angel, where did she go?"

He pointed to a forest in the distance. I stood quickly, walking closer to it. The grass tickled my legs as I walked.

The rain had stopped, leaving a deep, earthy scent heavy in the air.

Angel was stretching his wings out in an effort to dry them.

The gentle trickle of a creek reached my ears. Soon, the small water feature appeared. The woman sat beside it with her feet in the water.

"Who are you?" I asked, startling her.

"My name is Miriam."

"You said something about hope. What do you mean when you say I 'lost hope?'" I sat beside her, crossing my feet under me.

She smiled softly, her eyes lost in mine. Unseen memories danced in her gaze as she thought. I could almost see a story in her eyes. I leaned closer to her.

She nodded to herself before she began to speak. "Moses was my baby brother," she began. "When Pharaoh had an order made to kill the young boys, our mother hid him for as long as possible. One day, however, she could no longer hide him. She found a basket and put him afloat in the Nile."

I was lost in her words, imagining what it must have been like. I knew she must have been frightened for her brother.

"I led his basket part of the way to Pharaoh's daughter. Once he had made it there, I found Pharaoh's daughter and offered to find a nurse maid for the baby. She agreed, and I brought our mother. Mama got to raise Moses until he was five.

"You see, when I was a child, my people lost their hope. They lost their faith in God. There was a flood of tears and blood as Pharaoh ordered death on the children of my people. All we had, in the end, was a tiny speck of hope, just like a pale star on a cloudy night. After several years, our hope had failed more and more. Then Moses led our people to freedom." She nodded.

"So, all you had was hope? You didn't know what would happen next?"

"Do you know what happens next in your life?" she retorted.

"But your brother is famous," I reasoned, "and my family and I are just plain humans."

"We were just 'plain humans' then, too. You never know what the future holds when you have hope." She grinned at my angel who had come to get me.

I stood to leave, turning and waving to her. Angel gently pulled on my arm, leading me to the door.

"What was she doing here?" I asked Angel.

"Relaxing," he laughed. "Life was not always easy on these people. Rest is their payment."

I nodded, walking across the small field and to the white door. I opened it, taking the first step through it. I looked around. The golden path began to be laid out. I walked down it slowly, glancing around, still wanting to see something more than white or gold.

Angel playfully hit my arm with his wing. It was wet and left cold water dripping down my skin. I giggled and shoved him good-naturedly. For a moment, I forgot where I was.

Before I knew it, the next door was in front of me. It was open, waiting for my arrival. I stepped through, watching the white swirl away.

Chapter 10

I entered the room completely, carefully. It was lit with a dull, warm light. I noticed a stairway leading to a door on one side. A woman sat on a bed with red silk sheets in the middle of the room. Her back was turned to me. All I saw was her long, dark hair. She turned to me when she felt my presence, her deep brown eyes meeting my gaze.

"Lea," she greeted as she took my hand and sat me beside her.

"Who are you?" I asked.

"Delilah." Her eyes were sad as she spoke.

"Like Samson's hair, Delilah?" I looked back at Angel for the answer.

He nodded, looking back at Delilah to shift my attention to her.

Tears stained her dark eyes. She stood and made her way to a box in the corner of the room. She pulled a small blade from it. Walking back to me, she set it down.

"This is what I used, the blade I cut his hair with," she sighed.

"Why did you do it?"

"I was pressured into it," she began. "You see, Samson had humiliated my family, and they knew he loved and trusted me. They told me to cut his hair as he slept beside me. I knew it was wrong, yet I did it to please my family. I didn't know they would blind him."

"Did you ever truly love him?" I let the question hang in the air.

"I always have." She smiled sadly, taking the knife in her hand.

She grasped it tightly and, in her other hand, her hair. She slid the blade across her hair, cutting inches off. She left it short and uneven. A few tears fell as she cut, but she never once hesitated.

I stared at her in awe. "Why?"

"To move on," she said as she dried her tears.

I looked to Angel for advice, but he ignored my pleading eyes. He just nodded back towards Delilah. *Some help he is*, I sighed. I turned back to her, watching a faint smile drift across her lips.

"You have wronged one who loved you just for praise from a family member, a sister," she told me quietly.

"N-no, I haven't." I choked on my lie.

"Tell me the story." She let me rest my head on her shoulder.

"Well, his name was Mr. Williamson. He was a blind man who ran the concession stand at my sisters' high school when I was in elementary school. He was so kind to everyone. If I were having a rough day, he would always let me sit and talk it out with him. He was amazing," I sighed.

"Continue."

"My sister told me I was too good, told me I never did anything wrong in my life and that meant I never truly 'lived.' She told me I had to steal from Mr. Williamson if I wanted to be called her sister or hang out with her and her friends. I wanted to be accepted.

"So, I gave Mr. Williamson a fake dollar and took two candy bars instead of one. I knew it was wrong, but my sister and her friend were so proud of me. And I did it again. I don't know why I did." I sighed.

Delilah held me close as I sniffled. She patted my back gently. I could not hear a heart beating in her chest or the sounds of her breathing. But I felt the pressure of her arms against me. It was a slight comfort.

"Do you think Mr. Williamson would still accept you as you are?" She stroked my hair.

"I don't know why anyone would." I swiped away a few tears.

"You know, God will accept you in any form you take. He will love and forgive you." She let me sit up.

"I don't think He could," I sighed out.

"So many don'ts. How about changing a few to 'cans'? Mr. Williamson can forgive you and love you still. God and Jesus can and will love you forever and forgive you for all your sins. You just have to accept Him the way you want to be accepted." She smiled at me, a sparkle in her eyes.

I nodded uncomfortably; I did not believe what she was saying. I had to earn love. I had to earn forgiveness, and I just had not. There were no good things about myself buried in the depths of my mind, at least not that I could fine.

The door at the end of the stairway started to glow. I knew it was time to continue. I gave a "goodbye" wave to Delilah. As I left, I looked back and saw a tall, muscular man beside her, playing with her short hair. He kissed her softly and sat beside her. I knew she was forgiven. I knew she was loved.

Angel and I began the walk to the next room. We walked in silence for a moment before I spoke. "Angel?"

"Yes, sweet child?"

"When will I be home? I'm tired of all these new faces." I sighed softly.

"Soon but not just yet." He nodded to the door beginning to form in the distance.

I nodded, and we continued. As we reached the

next door, I walked through. The light annoyed me, but I waited as the room began to form around us. We were in a house like the one I had met Mary in. I walked to the chairs around the table to wait to the next person.

Chapter 11

A woman entered the room through a cloth-covered doorway. Her hair was pulled back in a braid. She looked surprised to see me but smiled.

"I was not expecting you so soon." She laughed softly.

She walked around the room, examining me from a distance. After she walked the perimeter of the hut, she went and sat across from me. She shooed Angel away with a glance.

He chuckled and walked from the room.

"This is girl time," she stated as I looked at her.

"So, who exactly are you?" I smiled awkwardly.

"Mary." She laughed at my confused expression. "The sister of Martha."

"Oh, where is your sister?" I looked around the room.

"She does not have a lesson for you; I do. However, if you are curious enough, she is talking to your angel outside."

I strained my neck to look out the window, seeing Angel talking with a woman who looked similar to the one before me. I smiled at Angel as he laughed with the woman.

"Alright then. What *is* your lesson?" I looked back at her.

"Take time to listen." She smiled.

"Listen to what?"

"Guess."

"God? Jesus? Angels? I don't know." I shrugged.

She shifted in her chair, trying to get comfortable. She looked at me with kind eyes, letting me mull over what I had said. Mary laughed as I looked down at my lap.

"Yes, dear child. You see, I was lucky enough to meet Jesus during my life." She looked at me with pride.

"I know that story. Your sister was lazy, and you did the right thing and did what you needed to." I rolled my eyes.

"You do *not* know my story then," she said flatly.

I started to speak, but she hushed me. She stood slowly and walked behind me, picking a flower from my braided hair. I had forgotten the flowers from Eve.

Mary handed me the small flower she had taken out. Sitting back in front of me, she smiled. She began to speak again, looking me in the eyes.

"Think before you speak, dear." She nodded, indicating that I should speak.

"Well, Martha just sat and listened to stories. She didn't do anything to help you. You had to do everything on your own," I reasoned.

"But Martha listened when I did not." She sighed.

"So? She should have helped."

"When Jesus came, I wanted to make sure everything was perfect for Him. Martha decided to sit and learn. When I confronted her, Jesus said she had done what was right: listening to the word of God. I was told to take more time to listen. I could do chores any day, but I could only listen once," she explained to me.

"But—" I started.

"No buts. You must understand. You only feel that I did the correct thing because something similar happened with your sister." She looked at me expectantly, waiting for me to tell the story.

"Well, my sister would always just listen to my great grandfather, Pops, instead of helping MiMi and me with the housework. It was annoying because he always acted like she did the right thing when I was the one who did the chores." I felt anger boiling up inside me.

"Calm down, Lea. She wanted to learn. Did she not learn how to whittle? Is that not something you wish *you* had learned? You see, sometimes, listening is more important than making things look nice."

I stood angrily and walked to the corner of the room. I did not want to listen to her. She was biased and only wanted me to listen to a God and Savior that I did not believe in.

She stood and walked to me, holding me close, swaying us both as we stood. She reached behind me, playing with my hair.

Mary brushed out my braid, setting the flowers from it in a small vase on the table as she walked away from me. I missed the sweet scent of the flowers, but I knew they would not stay in my hair for long.

"So," I started, "what you're saying is that I should stop and listen sometimes?"

"Indeed. Sometimes, it is best." She smiled.

"But what if stuff needs to get done?" I argued.

"Sometimes, my dear. Not all the time. Sometimes, things do need to be done. You just must learn what is appropriate. But always listen to the Lord." She spoke calmly.

I nodded, beginning to understand, though I was still hesitant to trust in "the Lord." I heard footsteps, and it startled me. Angel stood behind me and smiled.

"It's time to move on, Lea." He nodded to a door just outside the hut.

I nodded a goodbye to Mary before meandering out of the hut. Angel trailed behind me, so I stopped to let him catch up.

"Angel, what do you talk about with the people I don't meet?" I asked innocently.

"Different things, child. They all know me as I know them."

I nodded, walking beside him as we exited through the door. The golden path laid out in front of us once more. We walked in silence, listening to the same hum of the world.

He paused to open the next door for me, and I nodded in thanks to him. As I walked through the door, the new world appeared in front of me.

Chapter 12

We stood in a desert; small shrubs speckled the land around us. A woman walked to us out of the distance. She was older than the others I had met and was carrying a basket.

She set a blanket on the sand, setting the basket on top. Sitting down, she invited me to sit also. Angel sat beside me, flicking sand out of his wings.

She hummed softly, pouring us water as the sun beat down on us. I did not feel much heat, but some of it reached me. The woman had a head cover, trying to protect herself from the sun.

"Lea, how are you? And Angel, you as well?" She smiled.

"I'm doing alright, I suppose." I shrugged.

"I am well, Sarah." Angel nodded to her.

I looked at the woman. I knew there were a lot of Sarahs in the Bible, and I was not sure which this one was. I met her eyes as I tried to figure her out.

"I am the wife of Abraham," she explained.

I nodded, trying to remember her story, trying to think of what lesson she could be introducing me to. I looked at Angel for answers, but he just shook his head and motioned back to Sarah.

"You know, I met an angel once."

"Oh, was he anything like my angel?" I asked, pushing my angel's arm gently.

"Not quite. This angel was sent to give me a message, the news that I would become a mother in my old age."

"Didn't you? Wasn't your son 'The Father of Many Nations'?" I asked with wide eyes.

"Yes, but at first, I did not believe." She shook her head then looked out into the distance.

I followed her eyes. There, far away from us, I saw a mirage. Sarah was standing there with an Angel floating before her. His large wings stirred up the sand around them.

"You will have a child, Sarah," I heard him say.

Sarah laughed at him, shaking her head in disbelief.

I turned back to the real Sarah, the one sitting in front of me. "Why did you laugh at him?" I asked her.

"If you were old and had never had a child, would you have believed him?"

"I don't know. An angel is an angel. It'd be crazy to ignore one if you met one," I argued.

She and Angel looked at each other and began to laugh.

Angel shook his head and took deep breaths to steady his breathing. Sarah just shook her head at me.

"And here you are, surrounded by angels yet laughing off what they say. You ignore the angels *you* see," she chuckled.

I huffed and looked at Angel for support. He just shook his head. *That was helpful,* I pouted.

He shot me a glance, as though he had heard my thoughts again.

"Alright, Sarah. What do you suggest I do? Listen to total

strangers that I meet in a heaven-like place?" I snapped.

"Exactly. Yes." She smiled. "You are a smart girl."

I rolled my eyes at her. *This is unbelievable. I don't know where I am, and I am meeting people from the Bible. This makes no sense.* I growled internally. Then, I looked at Angel. His eyes were sad and disappointed.

I opened my mouth to talk to him, but no words came. I looked at Sarah; her green eyes met mine, filled with power. She stared at me.

"What do I need to do?" I finally asked.

Sarah smiled. "Just follow your heart and listen to the angels."

"How many angels will I meet?" I looked around as I spoke.

"Many more." She laughed. "Oh, and one more thing. Don't try to take God's will into your own hands. Sometimes, it's best for him to take control."

I gave her a quizzical look. She pointed back out into the desert. There, in the distance, I saw another woman I had not seen before.

"That was a maid of Abraham's. I let him sleep with her, thinking that was how Abraham would have children," she began. "Later, I fell pregnant. Then, I knew I had done wrong by trying to take control."

I shivered. *If God would have taken control of my life, everything would have been better for me. I would have been happier,* I groaned in my mind.

"That is not true, child. God has taken *some* control in your life. Otherwise, you might have completely died and not have woken up here." Angel talked me out of my thoughts.

"I just feel so helpless." I confronted my thoughts aloud. "Everyone I've met has this great story of their lives being changed, and here I am, just sad."

"You are here to learn, dear girl. God will help you with the rest," Sarah said, helping me stand.

I hugged her goodbye, waiting for Angel to stand, too. He brushed the sand off the tips of his wings, mumbling to himself. I laughed, watching him shake his wings out.

We walked side by side to the door. Sarah turned away and began walking in the opposite direction.

"Where is she going?" I asked Angel.

"Home, where her family is waiting." He smiled.

"Does she live in this desert?" I gasped.

"No," Angel chuckled. "She lives in heaven."

"Then where are we?" I asked, looking around.

"Just outside the gates," he explained, ushering me on down the path.

"Wait, really?" I looked around to try and find the pearly gates from the Bible.

"You will not see them, dear child," Angel chuckled.

I huffed loudly. Then, we reached the next room. I spun around, forgetting my frustration, and watching the white morph into grass that grew around me rapidly.

Chapter 13

A large hill developed. Two crosses sat with a space in the center. Where the third cross should be was a small hole in the ground. I felt a hand on my shoulder; it startled me. I turned quickly, seeing a man. His hair was a dull brown, but his eyes sparkled. He smiled at me shyly. There was an awkward moment in silence.

"My name is Shlomo." His words were barely audible.

"Hello." I smiled uncomfortably.

He was very shy, unlike the others I had already met. I looked around again, taking in the scenery. It was a desperate attempt to figure out who Shlomo actually was.

"Do you know what I am?" Shlomo spoke again.

"An angel."

"Yes." A hearty laugh shook him. "But I am a thief."

"A thief?" I asked aloud.

His face was tinged red with embarrassment, but he gave an unspoken "yes."

I looked around again. This man was strange, and I barely recognized his name. I turned to the crosses, a sudden realization hitting me.

"Which one were you?" I pointed to the crosses.

"Be humble, Lea. Know the Lord and ask for forgiveness." He spoke gently. "You may not know Him now, but one day, you will."

He turned me away from the crosses toward the horizon. The sun was setting in the room, casting brilliant colors out over the open space. Deep oranges and yellows fluttered through the growing darkness.

I looked at Shlomo. He looked to me. So many questions fluttered through my mind. *What does Jesus look like? Was Shlomo scared when he was on his cross? How did he know he was with Jesus?*

"You will know Him when you see Him." Shlomo answered one of my unspoken questions.

"Do I deserve to see him?" I asked shyly.

"Did I?" He shrugged in response.

"What is that supposed to mean?" I rolled my eyes.

Shlomo shook his head and sat on a nearby rock. He found a stick and began drawing in the dirt in front of him.

"You know, stealing is wrong. It is in the Ten Commandments not to. And yet, I did. I had no reason other than greed and jealousy. I got what I deserved, but that Man—the Man between my friend and me—He did not. He was innocent." Shlomo sighed heavily.

"What was he like?" I breathed softly.

"Magnificent. My name means peace, and in my life, I had not found any until I laid eyes on that Man. I found true peace in His presence. Even in the middle of pain, embarrassment, and suffering, I found peace in Him.

"I asked Him to remember me as He entered His kingdom. He told me I would join Him there. When the time came, they broke my legs. They broke my friend's legs. But they left His unbroken. He is the true Savior, then and now." He finished with a smile.

I felt a hand on each shoulder. Shlomo and Angel stood with me as we watched the sun be swallowed by the hills.

"Trust yourself to know Him and be humble in His presence." Shlomo spoke without looking at me. "In spite of the past, great things are to come. You will do amazing things, Lea. Remember that."

Another hand touched my head softly, but no words came, just a welcomed silence. I stood quietly, taking in the sweet scent around me.

"It's time to go," Angel said from beside me.

A door appeared behind us, as white as snow against the hills. Shlomo walked us to the door, opening it for us.

I looked past the door, seeing the moon trying to rise in the distance. Not a cloud tainted the sky. Angel and I walked through it together. I was growing tired of these meetings.

My angel must have noticed as he said, "I know, child. You are growing weary of the journey, but we must continue."

I nodded, walking with him to the next room, ready to return home. The path was longer ahead of us, and it seemed to lengthen with each door. The golden path paved itself further before us. I started speed-walking to get away from the never-ending purity.

"How many more people, Angel?" I asked hopefully.

"Quite a few." He chuckled.

"But I want to be home now," I whined loudly.

"Hush, child, and be patient. Everything will happen in its own time."

I slowed my pace, taking a deep breath in. *I'm here for a reason; no need to rush it,* I tried to reason in my mind.

Angel chuckled to himself and patted the top of my head

gently. In return, I stood on my toes to ruffle his hair. He just laughed as I stumbled.

He and I were just enjoying the others company. I suppose I was just happy to not be alone on this journey, but I was unsure as to why Angel enjoyed my company so much. I shrugged it off as we continued.

I wanted to ask him why he was with me on this journey, but I did not want to ruin the friendship we had. I was afraid to lose him. He made me feel like I was worth something.

We soon arrived at the door. Angel opened it for me,

letting me pass through first. I
thanked him, waiting to see how
this room would form.

Chapter 14

A large mountain grew before us as though the world was in a time-lapse. Its grey stone was dull in the sunlight. From further away, I heard a child talking to someone.

"Welcome her the way I welcomed you," a familiar voice said.

"Here she is," the young boy's voice rang. He stepped out from behind the mountain.

"Hello?" I looked down at him.

His skin was slightly tan, his eyes and hair brown. Smiling widely, he ran to me.

"Lea," he shouted as I caught him in my arms.

"Hello there." I looked at my angel for help, but he simply laughed. The small boy jumped from my arms, landing on his feet.

"My name is Matthias," he announced proudly, pointing to himself.

I looked at my angel once more for help.

"This is your journey, not mine," Angel chuckled, smiling playfully. I picked the boy up again, placing him on my hip.

"Well, Matthias, what can you teach me?" I asked, tickling his stomach.

His giggle made me think of my Jeremiah. My heart melted, the thought of my unborn son drifting into my mind. Matthias held on to me, looking toward the mountain top.

"When I was this age, this form I am showing myself to you in," he began, "I was walking through a crowd of five thousand men. They were all listening to a man, though I could not see him through the crowd."

"Oh, you were one of the five thousand that Jesus fed."

"Well, kind of," the boy chuckled. "You see, when my mother sent me with my father to listen to the man, she packed a lunch for me. Five loaves and two dried fish. By the time I went to eat it, it was getting darker."

I stared at the boy. I was in awe as he continued his story with a soft giggle and a wink to Angel.

"The disciples were worried about feeding the five thousand. They had no money, and there was no place to eat. They forgot who they were with. So, Jesus sent the disciples out to search for food. A nice man came by me, looking worried. He stopped when he noticed my meal. He introduced himself as Andrew and led me to the man whom I had heard talking all day.

"My first time seeing him was spectacular. He was magnificent, amazing—I can't begin to describe him—and he took my lunch and fed the entire crowd! He blessed the bread after he had taken it, and more bread kept coming from my basket. He blessed the fish after he had held it, and even more fish came. There was so much food that after everyone had eaten, they had more than twelve baskets of food left over to take with them." He smiled widely.

The boy started playing with my hair. I ruffled his playfully. Voices within me scolded me, and I held on to him tighter.

"Everyone is important. Everyone has a purpose with God," the small child said.

He is so mature.

He looked me in the eye, his gaze strong and aged with wisdom. "Even you have a purpose." His smile was crooked but full of character.

"I'm not sure if I believe that," I sighed.

"You may not know it yet, but you will one day." He spoke with a commanding tone.

I nodded as I sat him down carefully.

He ran away from me with a quick wave.

I noticed the sky. "Angel," I said, "wasn't it just sundown?"

"Each room is like a different day," Angel explained, walking me forward.

A door appeared in the mountain that Matthias had been hiding behind. I looked around the room one last time; the shiny blue sky was beautiful against the stone mountains. I shook my head and continued on.

We made our way through the shining white and walked the golden path. The next room was even further ahead than the last time. I held my angel's hand, soothed by the knowledge that I was not alone on this long journey. He tightened his grip, relishing the moment as though it would not last.

"Who's next?" I asked.

"Someone." He winked.

I huffed but continued to walk by his side. The path meandered around aimlessly in the white. It was boring at best, and the silence was overwhelming.

"I was wondering… How do you know all these people?" I asked cautiously.

"We all live in heaven together. It would be hard not to know them." He laughed to himself.

"Will I know them when I am in heaven?" I quizzed.

"Why wait? You already know them now." He nodded ahead of us.

The next door opened itself as I went to walk through. Angel followed closely behind me. I stood still as the misty white formed into beings.

I looked around for some sign of my home. Anything to comfort me. I searched desperately.

I was still a long way from home. Closing my eyes for a moment, memories of life danced through my mind. Everything felt so far away. Everything felt so fake. *Home,* I cried in my mind. *I want to be home.*

Chapter 15

The room shifted into a small pier. The salty scent of the sea drifted into my nose. I looked at Angel; he nodded and pushed me forward onto the dock with his wing. I walked cautiously, listening to the dock creak with age. Angel lifted my head.

"Don't look down," he instructed me. "The water is deep. It will frighten you."

By that point, I trusted Angel with my life. He obviously

had my best interests in mind, so I listened, focusing on the man sitting not far from me, his feet dangling into the dark depths.

I made my way next to him, sitting on the sharp wood. It stabbed at my legs.

"Lea, sweet girl, how are you?" the mysterious man asked.

"I'm alright." I shrugged.

He held his hand out to me. "Jonah." His smile was warm.

I accepted the introduction, taking his hand. It was rough in mine. He turned back to the water, staring out at it.

He opened his mouth to speak, but no words came.

Turning to me again, he spoke clearly. His eyes were lost as he began to tell his story.

I rolled my eyes, thinking I knew it all already.

"Nineveh," he started, "was the city I was called to go to. However, I did not think this city was worthy of being saved. So, instead, I boarded a boat and left in the other direction.

"The boat was caught in a storm during the night. The sailors began throwing all their precious cargo off the ship, hoping to stop the water intake. I saw these men crying, begging each of their own gods to help them. I knew only my God could.

"I explained what I had done, and out of hope for saving the ship, I instructed them to throw *me* into the water. As I began to sink, I prayed one last prayer, and a large fish came and swallowed me. I heard the men on the ship praising my God as the storm settled."

He paused for a moment, looking behind us. He pointed at a city in the distance. It was a large city, bigger than I'd expected.

"After three days of sitting in dark silence, after three days of not knowing where I was going, I was set free in a rather nauseating way." He laughed to himself before continuing. "I found myself on the shore of Nineveh. I prayed a prayer of thanksgiving. My God—*our* God—had saved me in more ways than one. I left for the city to warn them that in forty days, God would destroy their city.

"It took me three days to walk the city. Three days of proclaiming until their king heard me. He told his people to repent. And so, they did. They sat in ashes, wearing nothing but sackcloth. They fasted to please our God, and He let them live.

"I was devastated, I felt those people were still unworthy of being saved. Instead of staying and rejoicing with them, I built a shelter just outside the city and waited. God was gracious and let a plant grow for me to shade me from the harsh rays of the sun. Yet, I still complained.

"One night, God sent a worm to kill the plant. I sat in the hot sun for hours, asking God to kill me. He explained what he had done and why, and I was humbled," he finished.

I stared at the city in the distance. It looked beautiful and peaceful. Jonah sat with me in silence for a moment, taking in the waves and the smell of salt water.

"I ran." Jonah spoke with such anger and regret, breaking the peaceful silence. "I ran from the Lord. He wanted to use me to help others, but I just ran." His words grew louder.

I was frightened. I moved backwards, trying to get away from him.

"Do not run." His voice dropped to a whisper. "Do not be like me. Trust in Him."

I looked around. There was lightning in the distance of the dark, cloudy sky. Thunder echoed softly.

"If He wishes to use you for the betterment of the world, let Him."

A chill ran through me. *What if I already missed my chance?* I asked myself. The world seemed to float away, leaving me in the darkness of my own mind, alone. I felt a hand on my back.

"He will be with you," two voices said.

I knew one must be Jonah, and I had become accustomed to the other, familiar voice. I turned to look back, but no one was there. Shivering, I pondered who else could have been there.

Who else is here? Jonah touched my back, a smile across his face. He stood quickly, taking my hand. Helping me stand, he pulled me to him in a hug. He had no heat; it was as though he were not there. Then, my angel gently pulled me from him, walking me to the next door. It was behind where I had sat. It looked smooth compared to the pier.

We reached the door, and my angel opened it slowly. I walked through to find the golden path laid out before us.

"Angel?" I started another conversation to fill the silence.

"Yes, Lea?"

"Why am I here? On this journey?" I spoke without looking up.

"Ask me again later, dear child. We are here," he answered, opening the door before us.

"No. I need to know." I stopped before the door, blocking our way in. Angel looked at me, shock present in his eyes.

"Please, child. We must continue. I will explain later." His eyes pleaded with me to be reasonable.

With a sigh, I stepped through the door. This room had already formed before I had arrived. I looked around curiously.

Chapter 16

A rocky path came together before my eyes. Looking around, I spotted a tall man sitting on a nearby boulder.

"Paul." My angel spoke in a voice riddled with command. The man looked up from his Bible. Annoyance was clear in his eyes, but it melted away upon seeing me.

"Is this the girl?" His voice carried a joyful lilt.

My angel nodded at him.

The man bounced like a child.

Paul? I thought to myself. *The name is so familiar.*

My angel stepped away from me, letting Paul take the lead. He walked me down the winding rock path. "You think you are a sinner?" Paul asked me, arching one eyebrow.

"Well, yes."

"I am a sinner also. Much worse than you." He nodded.

I turned to Angel for an answer, and he just shrugged.

When I looked back to the man, Paul, he smiled. He shook his head as he laughed.

"Do you not believe me?"

I signaled a "no."

"Sweet, sweet child," he began. "I have harmed many people." He must have seen the bafflement prancing in my eyes. His aged eyes met mine.

"My name once was 'Saul of Tarsus'." He hesitated before continuing his story. "I tracked down those who followed Jesus. I was once a religious leader, and I followed the rules in every way I could. I hunted those who followed Jesus as I thought He was a fake. I was there for the death of a few of His followers.

"I remember the stoning of Steven well. He said, 'I see you Lord, and I am coming.' Though in the moment, I did not know what he meant.

"A while later, on the road to Damascus, a great light blinded me, and I heard Jesus speak. I felt love and sadness all at once, and I felt His great disappointment in me.

"I found myself no longer able to do what I thought was my calling. I was blind for quite a while, but while my eyes were closed, my heart was opened. And finally, as the Lord forgave me, He sent Ananias. The man was afraid of me, yet God encouraged him. Ananias came and blessed me, and as the water trickled down my face, I could feel forgiveness warming my soul.

"I was given back my sight. I could then go and tell the world what it meant to have God forgive you." He smiled at me.

"So, were you really blind?" I gasped.

"Yes. It was a difficult time for me, though I would not change what happened."

He touched the ground, whispering to it something, though I could not hear what. A small flower grew through the course dirt. "Thank you, Lord." He looked upward, toward the shining light. Then, he turned back to me, tears in his eyes as he plucked the flower and put it in my hair.

What if I am never forgiven for all that I've done? I asked myself. A chill ran through me. I feared the future then, blinded by the present.

"The Lord tells me what you think, and I believe you know the answer." Paul smiled softly to me.

I shivered. *There is no God, no greater being. This is just a dream.* I repeated that to myself a few times.

My angel had disappointment glowing dully in his eyes.

You are a disappointment, the voices whispered demonically in my mind. I stared at my angel, silently begging him to quiet them.

"I cannot do that, child," he huffed in despair.

I acknowledged it, annoyed by having to listen to them.

"Do not let them blind you, Lea," Paul called to me. "Are you ready to move on?"

I gave a dip of my head in response. He traced a door in the boulder. A bronze handle appeared. It sparkled like a new coin in the strange light. He turned it, letting the door begin to open.

Who will I meet next?

My angel beamed happily, knowing what I did not.

Clouds greeted me in the opening of the door. "Good luck," Paul shouted, shutting the door behind us.

"What happens when we leave a room?" I looked at my angel in question.

"They return to their angelic body, nothing a human's mind can handle. We choose the form of our life to make it possible for you to meet us," he answered softly.

"Come on." I shoved him playfully. "Tell me more."

His laugh was deep, but he stopped us. "An angelic form is either a ball of light with a halo or the form of a person in life with large wings and a halo of the Great Lord's love."

This made me realize I had not seen a single halo, not even on Angel. "Where is your halo?" I asked quickly.

"The halo of God's love is what the human mind cannot handle. His love is too great, too strong, and too pure," Angel explained with a smile.

"Will I have one?"

My question startled my angel. He paused, looking at me as though I had insulted him. "Everyone will. God loves all his children. He cries whenever one does not make it into heaven."

Does not make it to heaven… The words bounced around my brain.

"Does that mean—"

My angel bowed his head slightly.

I trembled. The thought of not making it to heaven frightened me.

The next room began to form around us. Sand materialized under our feet, and a rock grew in the distance. A light like the sun beat down on us as we walked towards a man sitting on the rock.

Chapter 17

I struggled to walk in the sand; it was loose and difficult to move in, so Angel held me as we made our way to the rock. I looked at the man closely. His skin was tan, and his eyes were a dark brown.

He looked up and smiled, patting the rock beside him, shifting over so I could sit with him. Angel stood beside me as the man began to hum a soft tune I did not recognize.

"My name is Job," he said.

"I'm Lea."

"So I have heard. Do you know who I *really* am? Do you know me?"

He chuckled.

"Job," I answered awkwardly.

He nodded and looked at the sand, drawing in it with his staff. He drew a large house with many people surrounding it.

I smiled at the drawing. "Is that your family?"

"Was." He sighed. "They all died before their time. I have a lesson for you, dear girl."

I looked at Angel, and he patted Job on the back.

Job smiled softly and took a deep breath. He looked at the desert around us and began his story.

"I was gifted many things by God: a big house, a large and loving family, many animals to keep us healthy and fed, and good health for us all," he started.

"So, let me guess. The lesson is about how great God treats you," I huffed.

Job laughed at that and shook his head. A tear ran down his cheek, yet his smile still stayed.

"God is great, yes, but that is not my lesson. You see, I did not know at the time, but Satan had met with God and told Him I was a good child. God agreed, but Satan said he could turn me against Him. God said as long as I did not die, Satan could take from me.

"It was a test, but I was not aware. In one day, I received many letters. I learned my family had died, my livestock had been taken, and I had lost everything I cared for. I shaved my head and tore my clothes in mourning. Boils grew on my skin, leaving me without my good health.

"A few of my friends came, each telling me I had sinned and that God was angry with me. I knew that was incorrect. I had tried to be a good and grateful child. They all told me to curse God's name and die.

"I *did* want to die, but I refused to curse my Lord's name. I began questioning everything."

He looked at Angel, who nodded for him to continue.

I watched Angel as he turned away from me. I brushed off his unusual behavior, turning to Job to hear the rest of his story.

"I wondered why I had been born, why things kept happening to me, why God judged people by their actions when He could so easily alter and forgive them. I was angered, but I did not curse Him.

"God asked me a few questions in return. He asked where I was when He created. He asked who had made the land I stood on and the seas I sailed on. He asked me many questions I knew I could never answer.

"I begged for forgiveness. I openly admitted my lack of knowledge and God's unlimited powers. And in return, God gave me the things I had lost, multiplied. I had a new and loving family, more livestock, a new home, and perfect health with a long life." He sighed at the memory.

I sighed, too, knowing I had questioned God a lot. I had asked many of the same questions Job did. I had questioned my life, my worth, and my entire existence. I had questioned why my mother had died, why life had been such a struggle when I always tried my best to be a good person.

Job put his hand on my shoulder. His smile was pure and warm.

Angel stood further back, not meeting my eyes. He turned slowly and smiled at me. He came to me and ruffled my hair. His eyes sparkled with a soft affection in them. I looked at him more carefully, there was a tear in his eyes. I dismissed it as I spoke.

"So, what exactly is your lesson, Job?"

"Do not curse His great name. Sometimes, bad things happen to good people, but you must understand that He still loves you." Job nodded ahead of him to where a large house stood, surrounded by many women and children.

Does He really love me? I asked myself sadly, believing He did not.

Job looked at me with soft, understanding eyes. He sat with me in silence for a moment. "He loves you more than you will ever know," he finally said.

"How do you know?" I whispered.

"Because He loves all His children, even the lost ones." He took my hand and gripped it tightly. Then, he gave my hand to Angel, who helped me stand and led me towards the large house. The front door turned white, a bronze handle shining in the brilliant light.

Angel walked me through it.

We strolled together down the small path. It was quiet. I

looked at the golden brick under my feet. It was so beautiful it looked fake. I stared at my reflection in it. Angel's reflection was glowing more than mine.

"Angel, why does your reflection glow?" I pointed to the ground.

"That is just a little bit of the light from my halo, dear child. It is the most you can see." He laughed.

"Has everyone I met had a hidden halo?" I asked, thinking about everyone.

"Yes, and everyone you will meet also." He smiled to me as he opened the next door.

I walked through and into the blank room. With a snap, we stood in a large field of lavender. A man walked down a path in my direction. He picked some lavender as he strode, bring it to me. The sight was magnificent. I watched the man come closer until I could see his features. He seemed so kind.

Chapter 18

The man in the distance walked to me, his long beard swaying as he plucked flowers from his field. When he reached me, he gave me the small bouquet he had made. I felt as though I knew him well.

"Simon the Zealot." He bowed. "Or at least that is what many know me by."

His smile was playful, comforting. He made me happy just by being nearby. I did not recognize his name, though.

"I am not mentioned in the Bible as often as some." His smile was genuine but pained nonetheless. He crouched on the path, examining a small butterfly as it fluttered past.

"He was never this calm," my angel teased.

I dismissed the words. "Why am I meeting you?" I quizzed Simon.

"That will come in time. First, sit. Have some tea." He sat on a blanket surrounded by the flowers.

I groaned but sat beside Angel. Simon gave us both a cup of tea. It smelled like the lavender field. I sipped at it, tasting sweetness and hints of honey. It relaxed me. I felt myself loosening up.

I closed my eyes and tilted my head back, taking in the sounds and smells around me. I heard birds singing and bees buzzing. I smelt the tea and the flowers. It all felt so gentle, like it protected me from all wrong that could happen.

I looked back at Simon. He smiled and began to speak. His words were soft and calm.

"I was a Zealot. We believed that the best way to win our rebellion was though blades and wars. I was there; though I may not be mentioned, I was there with Jesus. I saw him changing the world, not with knives and wars but with love and kindness, grace and mercy.

"I have always been one to demand action, but I learned something through Jesus: love is stronger than steel. It is love that saved my life," he finished.

"Is this a 'love your neighbor' type thing?" I asked him with a sigh.

"Not quite. It is more of a love and forgive instead of fostering hatred for the world. You must learn to love others, even if you feel they do not deserve it."

"But what if they are mean to me?" I huffed.

"Love them." He smiled.

"What if—" I started.

"Love them," he interrupted me. "The answer is always love. Let God handle them. Just love them the best you can, and the Lord will take care of the rest."

"But why?" I started to argue.

"How do you get into heaven, dear girl?" Simon smiled.

"Through God's love and forgiveness, right?" I shrugged.

He nodded and stood. Looking out over the field, he paused then looked back at me. "You know how to get into heaven. Good. Do the other people in your life know?"

"I'm not sure," I said softly.

"Then make it your goal to teach them. You see, I was radical; I was sure that death was needed to prove a point. But Jesus taught me that love was always the answer. Teach those around you that love is the answer. Teach them to forget their twisted ways and live by the Lord's way," he explained quickly.

"I can try," I offered.

He smiled and accepted what I said happily. Walking around me, he traced a door in the air. Soon, the light door appeared, and the silver handle twisted to open the door for me.

"She will do well," I heard Simon whisper to my angel.

He nodded and smiled.

I held to my angel's hand, walking with him to the door. We stepped through and walked down the winding path to the next room.

"Who will be next, Angel?"

"Just wait, child, and you will see." He did not look at me, his eyes set on our destination as we walked the distance.

I stared at our feet as we walked side by side. I wondered if I would ever make it back to Earth and if I really wanted to go back. Angel must have known something was bothering me as he held my hand tighter and smiled down at me.

I looked up at him and asked again, "Angel, are there sinners in heaven? Have I met any *real* sinners?"

"Dear girl, ask me again later," he said with a smile.

I looked at him angrily but walked with him. I wanted to know soon, everyone on this journey seemed sinless. I knew there was the petty sins, those I felt like did not matter. I wanted to know more about worse sinners.

We walked through the door and the room opened up around us. I waited patiently for the room to take its shape.

Chapter 19

As we entered the room, a small field formed around us. A fruit tree stood over the man I was to meet as he read a book. Angel walked up beside him, smiling. The man noticed the extra shadow as he looked up. He laughed some at seeing my angel. Standing, he shook Angel's hand roughly.

"My name is Nathanael, though I have also been called

Bartholomew." The man nodded at me.

I smiled, dipping my head in introduction. "My name is Lea."

"As I have heard." He looked back at Angel.

I decided to hurry things along. I knew I was getting close to going back home. While the thought scared me, it was more of a comfort to imagine a happy world waiting for me back on Earth.

"Alright, Nathanael. What do you have for me to learn?" I smiled.

"Wait, dear child. It will come in time." He sat back under the shade of the tree.

He looked up, taking in the sun with a soft smile on his face. He breathed slowly as though to take in each scent the world had to offer. His brown eyes turned orange in a spot of sun. He seemed lost in thought, looking back on his life.

He smiled again, though I had not spoken. With a nod, he leaned back against the tree, his book in his lap. Looking around, he smiled at Angel. My angel nodded at him as though to convince him to break our silence.

"I used to sit under a fig tree very similar to this one. You see, in my time, fires were kept going in the house to cook, even in summer. It was often very hot. Fig trees were planted near homes to provide cool shade, and you could usually find me there, studying. All of my scriptures I read under the tree. I prayed to my God; it was where my heart was opened to Him.

"My friend, Phillip, came to me one day, saying he had met an important person, someone we should praise. He told me Jesus of Nazareth was the Savior. I scoffed, saying there was no way anything good could ever come from Nazareth.

"Then, I met Him. He told me He'd seen me under the fig tree. I knew it was impossible; He was a far walk from where I had sat. I knew He meant He'd seen my heart, seen me studying and praying. I knew I'd met my omniscient Lord." Nathanael was lost in his memory.

We sat for a moment, not speaking to one another. A fig was shining above his head. It looked beautiful and delicious. I stared at it for a moment, thinking.

"What is your lesson?" I finally asked softly.

"Ah, yes. I was waiting for you to ask again. My lesson is simple. Believe that you have an omniscient Lord. Believe that your God and Savior knows you. He knew you before birth, He knows you in life, and He will know you in everlasting life." He looked up to the sky.

"How are you so sure?" I prodded.

"Because He knew me under the fig tree. He knows you now. He knows your Jeremiah here, before birth. He knows your family here, after death. He is a God of love and compassion." He chuckled as he explained.

"So, you're saying he knows everyone in every stage of their life?"

"Yes. That is correct." He looked at me happily.

I nodded slowly. I was not sure if I truly believed him.

Angel sighed, knowing my thoughts. He was not frustrated, rather disappointed.

I looked at him with apologetic eyes, and he nodded to me with a slight smile.

"You know, the Lord knows you even when you do not yet know Him." Nathanael did not look at me as he spoke.

"I've heard, but it feels like I'll never know Him the way I should. Like, how can I find my way to Him?" I sighed.

"Everyone has a different story of their way to the Savior. Maybe this is yours." He winked as he stood.

He led me around the other side of the fig tree. He gave me a fruit, letting me take a bite. The sweet nectar dribbled down my chin. I wiped it off on my arm. Then, we walked further around the tree, and I saw the door.

I walked to it with Angel. He took my hand as he led me through. There was a cool breeze between Nathanael's room and the next. I let it blow through my hair.

I looked up at Angel, trying to think of another question to ask. I enjoyed finding out little things about heaven and angels.

"Does God actually know *everyone* that's ever lived?" I questioned as I walked backward to face him.

"Of course. He is the Creator. He knows and loves all. As Nathanael said, He is omniscient." Angel chuckled as I stumbled.

I nodded, turning back around and walking a little faster. I regretted asking the question and felt uneasy after the answer. I truly did not believe what he said, and I hated that he just repeated Nathanael. I thought back to the man; he had such a strong belief when I felt I did not believe at all.

"Nathanael did not believe at first. It may take some time before you do." Angel smiled.

He put his hand on my back to walk me closer to the next door. I looked at it, knowing I had more to meet. I took a deep breath in and walked through.

Chapter 20

As we reached the room, I saw a figure. The new man stood in a garden, near a cave with a large rock. We walked to him, and he turned to us.

"Welcome," he greeted.

I sat beside him on a small bench.

"I am James the Lesser."

I dipped my head respectfully to him.

"Son of Alphaeus, descendant of one of the original twelve tribes. My family was a kind of 'old school' family, as the people would say nowadays. But that is enough of that. I wanted to tell you about something in my life.

"Shortly after being called to follow Jesus, the twelve—myself included—were sent two by two to various towns. We preached, healed, and cast out demons. I saw many miracles on these journeys. Then, once returning to Jesus, I saw many more."

I listened patiently, though a questioned poked at me. He

must have noticed as he smiled and nodded for me to ask it.

"What are you going to teach me?" I felt the question prick in my throat.

"Be calm." He chuckled softly. "It is nothing you could not teach yourself."

I felt my cheeks warm as I began to blush in embarrassment.

"No need to be embarrassed, child. You *are* here to learn." My angel's warm voice floated through the wind.

"I was there, seeing the great Lord after He rose." James' eyes shined with the memory playing through his mind. "He was glorious," he breathed out. "His cloak was whiter than the clouds. His eyes held power and beauty."

I felt chills trickle down my spine. "Will I meet him?"

My angel shrugged at my question, a knowing deep within his forest eyes.

I turned back to James, staring at him, trying to make sense of his words. I finally asked, "What am I here to learn?"

James turned his sight towards the sky. "To believe." His words caused the birds to hush. Only the tinkle of water streaming somewhere in the distance could be heard.

"To believe what?" I trembled, causing my words to shake.

"In the truth of the Lord. To believe the miracles you see with your eyes."

I pretended to understand what he meant.

"You have seen the miracle of birth and death, no?"

I signaled a yes.

"Good. You have seen the works of the Lord." He paused, and the bird song returned. "Do you believe the Lord created all that you see that is good?"

This question I answered truthfully. The word stuck in my throat like the pills I'd taken had, though I had no water to push it down. "No." The word was barely audible.

My angel sighed.

James stroked at his small beard. "Do you believe that flowers bloom?"

"Yes," I laughed.

"Have you seen a flower born in the desert?" His words rang loudly in the near silence.

I had before. I nodded to him.

His smile reappeared. "You have witnessed a miracle!"

I chuckled at him as he walked around the tree. He plucked a small fruit from it then tossed it to me.

I fell backward, catching it, laughing at myself as he helped me up.

"Were you hurt?" His smile was wide as he asked.

"Not at all." I shrugged.

He jumped up on the bench. "Another miracle, here before you."

I began to understand. "Everything is a miracle?" My eyebrows furrowed in thought.

"You understand now!" my angel answered gleefully.

A warm excitement bloomed in me. "Everything is a miracle," I repeated, skipping through the garden. My shoes slid off, and I relished the cool grass between my toes. I felt like a child again.

James ran, slowing to a halt beside me, taking my hand. A seriousness now tainted his gaze.

He sat me down and began to tell me another story. "At what is now called the last supper, the

Lord told the twelve of us that there was a traitor amongst us. I was furious; hate pulsed through me. But I got to witness a great miracle because of it.

"Before the miracle, however, we all had to hide, afraid for our lives. As much as I was furious in that moment, as much as I hated the traitor, I ran from the Lord to protect myself. In the upper room, the dark and damp loneliness we hid in, the light of the Christ shined through. I witnessed Him alive again, but there was still a greater miracle: He loved us still, just as He loves you. Sometimes, bad things come before the good. There is just a wait."

I understood and gave a soft smile. James helped me to stand then led me further into the garden. Angel met us there. As I stopped, a door appeared on the large boulder near the cave. James opened for it for us. He waved a farewell to me as I pranced through with my angel.

"Goodbye," I shouted as he closed the door. Joy still circled in my being. We walked down the usual path to the next room.

I was growing tired of the white again, yet joy still pricked at me. I was happy, and that distracted me from the growing distance.

Angel and I kept a steady pace. I heard him start humming, and I recognized the song in an instant. It was a hymn, my grandfather's favorite hymn. I laughed at the fond memories that came to mind.

Angel chuckled and tapped me with his wing.

I ruffled a few feathers to annoy him, but he just laughed and flapped his wings to fix them. The breeze from it felt nice. He batted at me with his wing again in return. We laughed as the cycle repeated.

The door opened as we arrived in front of it. I walked through happily, waiting to see who was next.

Chapter 21

A waterfall blasted into the pool beside me. Pastel colors formed a rainbow in the spray. Large pines rimmed the pool. A man was leaned against one, his hair longer than the others I had met. He looked at me, motioning for me to come sit with him. So, I sat beside him against the tree.

"Hello, Lea," the man said. His voice was deep and warm. "My name is Simon Peter." He had a commanding air about him.

In my head, I was shot into my childhood Sunday school room, learning of him. One of the "fishers of men." He was the rock of the church. It felt odd to me, meeting such a devoted man, when I had not prayed in years. He met my eyes as I stared at him.

"You must long for your learning," he guessed.

"Very much so." I felt heat on my face.

"Lay back," he commanded me.

I did; the tree was rough against my back. He stood and walked in front of me. Walking to the water, he cast out his fishing nets.

I was frustrated, thinking the lesson he had for me would be to bring others to the Lord when I was not sure if *I* were with Him yet. What good would I be if I could not even convince myself He was real?

Peter walked back to me, sitting down beside me. He thought for a moment, and a heavy silence fell over us, only being broken by the sounds of nature.

"My brother, Andrew, and I were fishing when we first met the Lord. We were angry. We had not caught any fish that day. A man came to the shore and told us to cast our nets on the other side of our boat. And as we did, the nets filled with so many fish, we could not lift them into our boat.

"I knew who this man was. I told Him to leave me as I was a sinful man. Yet, this magnificent man told me I was to be a fisher of men for Him.

"On the way to Caesarea Philippi, I was renamed Peter; my name now means 'rock.' Jesus told me He would build His church on the rock. He renamed me after I told Him I knew He was the Messiah. He seemed proud of me in that moment. But moments never seem to last." He sighed.

"But what is your lesson for me?" I asked loudly.

Peter and my angel laughed together. "Dear child, sit and listen," my angel advised.

Peter looked at me once more. "My lesson is not of the Lord Himself but a lesson I have learned as well." His words were heavy with grief and regret.

What could it be? My thoughts came in a near silent voice in my head.

He shook his head slowly. "Do not deny what you love." He hung his head in shame.

I was fully confused until he spoke again.

"I denied my Lord—the one whom I loved most—just for warmth in the cold night. He died for everyone, yet I did not so much as shiver for Him."

I felt chills run up my arms. *Did he regret it so much as to dwell on it forever?* I turned to my angel to see if he had heard.

"No, child. He just sees a lesson in it," he explained.

"You have turned your cheek from the one who has always loved you. Turn back to Him." Peter helped me to stand, tightening his grip on my hands. "Promise me, Lea, that you will not deny Him like I have."

My throat constricted as though to strangle me. His eyes begged me to listen and do as he'd said. I did the only thing I could in the moment: I cried. I laid my head on his shoulder and sobbed.

"I have sinned many times, Lea. As have you. We are sinners alike."

I stared at him. This man—the rock of the church—stood before me and said we were alike. I did not believe. Peter was flawless, sinless, to me. I shook my head to argue.

"We are nothing alike!" I reasoned.

"Yet we are. Family and sinners, my dear, Lea. We are all made by the same great God. We are all sinners, tempted by pleasures and demons," he spoke.

I shook my head in disbelief. I was not ready to accept the fact that I was anything close to being like Peter, or anyone in Heaven. I looked to him as he told a new story.

"At the last meal with our Lord," he began, "He said there was a traitor. I refused to believe it. I was ready to kill whomever it was. I was ready, blade in hand, when they came for Jesus. I remember my sinful pride as I said I would follow Him to my death. He told me I would deny Him before the rooster crowed.

"I was in disbelief. But as the night came, He was right. I held my sword in my hand and wondered if I should be the one to die."

I stared at him. I did not know his story like this. I knew he had denied Jesus, but I never knew he had regretted it that much. His eyes were soft with sadness, but he kept his head high.

"Be calm and learn to trust in Him. Do not deny Him." Peter's voice cracked with sadness.

My angel's hand grasped my shoulder lightly then, pulling me to look at the door.

"It is time to go," he mouthed silently.

I held his hand like a child as he led me to the door that was slowly appearing. The handle shone in the light, causing a rainbow to appear. I turned back to see Peter pulling at the net, not struggling alone. In that moment, I swore I saw another man with him, helping him, though his back was turned toward me.

My angel walked me down the golden path to the next room. I was reminded of how weary I was of the same path every time. He must have noticed as he waved his arm. The walls became like the sea, small creatures swimming by. I applauded him, happy to see the change.

I stared at the fish and turtles as they surrounded me. It was beautiful. I had never seen the ocean, only fish in aquariums. The sight was awe inspiring.

He chuckled lightly as the sea-like walls diminished into nothing more than a cold room. A gentle wind blew past me, causing the room to form a shore. I took a deep breath in. The air was fresh and salty but welcoming as a soft mist tickled my face.

Chapter 22

A man sat on the edge of a boat, his feet on the small pebbles of the shore. He looked up at me slowly, standing to greet me.

Nodding to Angel, he shook his hand vigorously before taking my hand gently and walking me away from Angel.

"I am Andrew the Bringer to most," he began immediately. "I am here to teach you the lesson I learned."

I was slightly uncomfortable at his eagerness.

"Fear not. He will not hurt you," my angel called from behind me.

My breathing calmed like the sea beside me as I took deep breaths. As we walked to the boat, Andrew helped me into it. We left my angel on the shore as we floated out to sea.

"What will you teach me?" Impatience grew like a weed within me.

"First," he began, "you must know who I am. My brother, Peter, was the rock of the church. My brother got to perform a few miracles; I never really did. But I was important, nonetheless. I worked for the Lord. My greatest gifts were my ability so see the best in people and bringing them to the Lord. When something needed to be done, I tried to do it.

"When people needed to come to Jesus, I was often the one who brought them to Him. I was not like my brother; I made no bold statements. But I was always available to help others. You may have even met the young boy I took to the Lord to help feed the hungry five thousand."

"You are the one who brought Matthias to Jesus?" I gasped.

He chuckled and nodded. At that point, so many questions filtered through my mind. *If he was the one who brought Peter to Jesus, what would have happened if he didn't? If this man in front of me sees the best in everyone, what does he see in me? Those eyes have seen thousands of people and brought them to Jesus. Maybe he can help me get to Him, too.* The thoughts raced around my mind.

"My lesson is to bring others." His eyes met mine, filled with a deep respect.

How could someone respect me? I begged for an answer in my mind.

Pushing past that, I continued, "What do you mean?"

"Bring others to the Lord. My brother and I brought many to Him, and you can, too."

"I'm not even with Him yet," I snapped. His eyes sparked with disappointment. Part of me hurt in seeing it.

"You know not of yourself." He held tighter to my hand. "You are closer to Him than you believe."

I pulled away sharply.

"Please, Lea, listen to me." His words were sprinkled with concern.

"No," I cried. "You're supposed to bring *me* to Him."

"I need you to listen. The Lord never left you."

I covered my ears as the voices in my head grew louder. *Jesus never loved you,* one growled. *There is no God,* another laughed. I squeezed my eyes shut tightly.

"It is okay, Lea. He is with you even now."

I felt serenity crash over me like ocean waves. I opened my eyes to see a shining light beside Andrew, one so magnificent I felt the world stop. I blinked my eyes rapidly. When I reopened them, only Andrew was there. I took a deep breath in, letting it out slowly.

"Bring others to Him," Andrew repeated.

"But what do I do? I can't even seem to believe in Him," I sniffled.

"Do what you feel is right. You will believe in time." He smiled softly.

Andrew began rowing us back to shore as though he sensed my understanding.

I stared at him, amazed at how he had helped me feel so

strong. He shook his head some before speaking.

"It wasn't me who made you feel so strong," he said.

"Then who was it? Angel was on the shore. Only you and I were in the boat," I thought out loud.

"You will figure it out later," he smiled.

Once we scraped into the shore, my angel helped me from the boat. Andrew traced out a door, opening it for us.

"I hope I have helped you, Lea." His smile was faint.

I hugged him quickly; I felt closer to the Lord in that moment than I had all my life.

My Angel had already passed through the door, and I ran after him, still in awe of the underwater scenery. He grinned as I stared at the fish swimming by. *I love the ocean*, I sighed happily inside.

Everything was so calm. I loved every second of it. Finally, though, I had to break the silence. "Angel?" I began.

"Yes?"

"Why are these people meeting me?"

"Jesus knows you and knows you need the help. Accept it. Learn to follow what they say," he explained.

We walked along side each other in silence the rest of the way to the next room. Each time a thought came into my mind, the words never seemed to come. I dropped the prospect of a conversation.

I walked through the new door slowly, expecting a great world to grow before me. I looked around hopefully.

The next room opened wide at first before forming into a smaller room. It was brown with many windows covered by cloth. It would have been empty if not for a large table covered with papers and a cloth laying on the floor. A man sat at the table, looking up from papers to meet my gaze. He stood slowly, grunting with effort, and started coming towards me.

Chapter 23

"I am Matthew, renamed by the Lord." He brushed his hair out of his face with his hand. "I was once Levite, a tax collector. I worked for the Roman government, and for that, many people hated me. I added to their taxes so I could make more money for myself. I was very greedy.

"I was a businessman, more so than the rest. I invited Jesus to a party with the religious people of the time. They made fun of Him for eating with sinners like myself. But He said He had come to help the sinners.

"I wanted to record everything Jesus said and did. I was impressed most by the sermon on the mount. I felt as though my job was to prove to the world who Jesus truly was."

"You were a tax collector?" I asked, restating to clarify.

"Yes. I wronged many people. I took money from the needy." His voice was riddled with regret. He looked at the papers splayed out in front of him. Pictures of women, men, and children covered them.

"Who are they?" I asked him softly.

"The ones who need the Lord. I watch the needy now. I try to help right the wrongs of people like myself." He held up a photo of a man I recognized from the street that always sat by a local bakery.

I had never known his name, but I knew who he was. He was kind to everyone. His long, grey hair and beard were often ungroomed, but he always smiled. To everyone who passed him, he told, "God bless you in every way."

I thought back to him and his dog. He shared everything with his pet. If anyone gave him food, he would pray with them then split the food and give half to his dog.

I turned back to Matthew to hear more of what he had to say. His eyes were dark with sadness. I nodded for him to continue.

"This man will die in the coming winter if he does not find shelter. It stabs at my heart, seeing such a kind man treated poorly."

My stomach knotted. "Is that true?" I gulped as I turned to see my Angel. He nodded, looking away and out through a window. *That's horrible.* I shook the thought off.

"What am I here to learn?" I asked Matthew desperately.

"To help those in need when you can." He smiled, setting the picture down.

"What do you mean 'when you can?'" I tilted my head in question.

"Can you help a man stand when you cannot?" he retorted.

"Of course not." I shook my head.

"Then what makes you think you can save others when you have not yet saved yourself?" he shot back.

"But Andrew said I should bring others to Jesus," I argued.

"Ah, yes. Good. Start with yourself." He winked. "You are here to learn to find your faults and work to fix them."

My faults were many; I just refused to see them.

"What do you mean?" I asked him.

"Every being has faults, things that make them flawed, makes them less than perfect." He met my gaze. His eyes were tired but full of wisdom.

It shook me. This man knew so much, and there I was, lost and sad with so many flaws I had taught myself to ignore. The voices started up in my mind again: *You don't have flaws. You are a flaw. Even if there was a Lord, He would never want you. Useless. Worthless.* I began to cry, fighting what they were saying. *I am wanted. I am loved,* I repeated to myself.

My angel nodded at me. "Thank you for fighting them."

I let out a sigh in response. I looked for the door, ready to move on.

"The only way to move on is to truthfully say you will change," Matthew said to me.

The "truthfully" part was the hard part. I knew how to better myself, but I did not want to. I had to seek out help.

"I will," I lied.

Matthew shook his head while my angel bowed his.

"Lea," Matthew began, "be honest."

"I can't." I felt helplessness grasp me like cold hands. "I'm too scared."

Mathew held my hand, pulling me in for a hug. "Walk through the shadows with the Lord. He will be your light."

My light, I thought to myself. *I won't be alone in the dark.*

"Will you *try* to better yourself?" My angel repeated Matthew's question.

"I will." Those words gave me so much power. I felt invincible for that moment. Then, the door appeared before me.

I was beginning to understand the journey. It left a dull joy in the depths of my spirit.

My angel led me through the next door.

"Angel?" I did not look him in the face. "Is there really a God? Is Jesus real?"

"That is for you to decide, child," he replied, keeping a steady forward march.

I huffed but was glad to decide on my own. I looked ahead, the next room in reach.

I paused for a moment, putting my hand in the water wall of the ocean. It was cool to the touch, one of the few temperatures I felt there. I enjoyed it.

I smiled as small fish swam up to my hand. They swam easily through the water. They were beautiful.

Angel grasped my hand, walking me forward and through the next door. The room began to lay out before us.

Chapter 24

Once more, we were on a shore. It had fine sand instead of pebbles. There was a small dock with a boat tied to it. My angel led me over to the man sitting on the dock, mending his nets.

"Hello?" I shouted to him from a distance. He turned sharply, obviously startled. He smiled at seeing my angel and me, though. He stood quickly, racing to us.

"Hello, Lea!" He bounced on his toes.

I smiled uncomfortably.

"Oh, dear. I am sorry. You have no idea of who I am."

He bowed exaggeratedly, kissing my hand. Then, he straightened, motioning for me to come to the boat.

I looked to my angel for advice. He gave a short nod, and with that, I followed the man to the boat.

"You never told me your name," I mentioned.

"Oh, yes! My name is John, the brother of James."

I was excited for a moment, remembering the "Sons of Thunder." I opened my mouth for a question, but he hushed me. He handed me a net, taking one himself, and showed me how to mend it; we began working together.

"My father was Zebedee," he began. "My brother and I left him on the boat with the hired hands when we left to follow Jesus. That was wrong in my culture. Many generations often lived together in one house. And I left my father. I lost most of my family's love because of that, but I made a new family. The family I had with Jesus and the others was so real, I thought we had all been brothers all our lives.

"I was called 'the beloved disciple,' as Jesus and I were very close. I sat beside Him at the last supper. After He had risen, I was one of the disciples who ran to the tomb to search for His body."

"That's all well and good, but what am I here to learn?" I sighed.

"We will get to that." He smiled.

I stared at the net as I helped him mend it. It felt strange, sitting next to him, yet it was still comforting. I took in a deep breath and released it slowly.

"You have much to learn."

I looked at him in confusion.

"Lea, you have not stopped and followed He who cares for you." His words stung, but only because they were the truth.

"I dropped all I had and left for the Lord. You would have done the same in your youth, yet now you barely speak of His great name."

I felt the familiar glowing of my cheeks.

He chuckled sweetly. "It is normal, Lea. Not many have seen Him in life. I was one of the lucky few."

I smiled a dull smile as he spoke.

"I wish I could have known you in life." His words were nearly silent. "I could have taught you His way."

It felt abnormal, having someone seem to want to help me, yet the feeling became a comfort to me. I began to laugh. *What is becoming of me?* I felt tears streamed down my cheeks as I laughed. John joined me, holding me, his arms around my shoulders.

"What can become of us sinners?" he laughed aloud.

I held on to him as I cackled, my eyes streaming tears. I tried to calm myself, catching my breath. I wiped my face, grinning at John.

"Now, my lesson for you, dear girl, is to not delay in answering God's calling." He smiled.

"What do you mean?" I asked, still drying tears.

"God is calling to you. Listen and do as He says. You will do great things, Lea."

"Thank you for all of this," I said to him.

"I have done nothing; it was all you and the Lord." He turned before continuing to mend his net, watching me go back towards my angel.

"Angel," I shouted happily.

He turned to me, a welcoming gaze drifting over his face. He moved to the side, revealing a new door. I bounced with excitement. He opened it, letting me walk through first. I brushed my hand across the watery walls of the path.

"Could we have a tulip field?" I asked hopefully.

He nodded to me. Moments later, a field of yellow tulips appeared. I saw the next room in the distance. It felt as though the paths were getting longer still between each door.

My angel covered me with one of his white wings. He was the only one I had met who had the iconic symbol of an angel.

I brushed my fingertips over the feathers gently. They were beautiful. He flinched slightly but did not protest.

A light breeze blew across us. It had the scent of flowers and rain. It reminded me I was in heaven—or nearly there.

We walked together, his wing protecting me from something, though I was not sure what. All I knew was that I felt loved. I felt like I was wanted, needed even, something I did not feel on Earth. I held on to Angel's hand, knowing that when I did get home, he might not be there with me.

I dismissed the sad thoughts, turning back to the room which seemed much closer. Angel moved his wing and let the

sun shine on me. The next room
opened before us.

Chapter 25

The light from the shining tulip field darkened. A star-speckled sky grew above me. The tulips shrunk into small blades of grass. The next man laid in the field, staring up to the heavens.

My angel gently pushed me forward, so I walked to him cautiously. "Sir?" I called out.

He sat up sharply, relaxing when he saw my angel and me.

"Phillip, this is Lea." My angel shook his hand roughly.

Phillip turned to me, smiling widely. He walked me a little way across the smooth meadow. "Are you prepared?" he asked me.

"Prepared for what?"

"To listen and learn." He nodded once.

"I was first a disciple of John the Baptist. My friends and I were listening to him as he taught us when Jesus came. I went to my friend, Bartholomew, to bring him with me to see Jesus.

"You see, I was very invested in finding the nature of God and

Jesus, the Father and Son. I wanted to know Them personally. I wanted to know Them in a meaningful way."

I stared at him, confused. I was not sure what this man was talking about. I thought everyone knew God in a "personal way." I tilted my head to one side.

"You are confused, yes?" He smiled.

"Very."

"Everyone has a personal way of seeing God. Every person has a way they see Him, an individualized view. You must sit and pray, talk to Him, learn His ways, anything to help you experience Him in the truest way possible," he explained.

I shook my head. I did not know what my view of God was. I was not sure if I ever would. I sat down in the grass, playing with the longer pieces.

I tried to think of an answer quickly, something just to blurt out in hopes of it being correct. I felt a hand on my shoulder, and I looked back to see Phillip.

"You cannot force it, Lea. I was lucky enough to meet Jesus in person. I could see how He reacted to things. I saw my Lord and His love in person. So, tell me… Do you think you can know Him in minutes?"

"Shouldn't I?" I looked at him with sad eyes.

"Of course not. It took me years to know Him and see Him the way I do. It took me years to understand the way that *I* see Him." His voice held understanding in it.

"Then what can my answer be? If I can't know Him now, when will I? How do I move on from this room without understanding?" I bombarded him with questions.

"Well, your answer is not immediate. Nor can it be. As for your second question, time will answer it for me. You can move on from this room with the knowledge that everyone sees God differently. Some see Him as the angry God of Israel, and some see Him as the loving Father of Jesus. It is your choice on how you see Him," Phillip explained as he sat beside me again.

I sighed and laid back in the grass. I was not happy. In all the other rooms, I'd understood the lesson. I could give an answer that moved me on. But in this room with Phillip, I could not.

I watched the stars as they twinkled. I saw a few clouds float between them and me. I took in the sounds of crickets around me.

"Phillip?" I started.

"Yes, dear girl?" He looked at me.

"Why can't I find an answer for you?" I huffed.

"There is not an answer *for me*, only for you. You must ask yourself how you see Him. You need to pray and think for your answer." He smiled softy.

I nodded and stood. I stretched, then looked around for Angel. He was not far from me, standing beside a door. Phillip stood and came up beside me. The grass tickled my ankles as we walked with one another. Once we had reached the door, he opened it. Angel and I walked through it, returning to the tulip field.

I brushed my hands across a few magnificent flowers. I stopped to smell one, relishing the warm sun on my back and the welcoming scent of the bloom.

My angel ushered me onward, placing his hand on my back. The next room was far off in the distance. I paused on the path, turning to him.

"Who am I to meet next, Angel?"

"That is for you to learn."

I began to feel annoyance pricking at me. Inside, I begged to know.

I took in a deep breath, urging myself to calm as I let it out slowly. *Anger gets you nowhere*, I reminded myself. I waited for the voices to argue, for their demonic sounds to bounce around my mind, but nothing came. I relaxed a little, happy with their silence.

I played with the flower that was still in my hair. Its petals were as soft as silk. There was such a calm feeling in that place. I was slowly starting to love the feelings I had there. The love and comfort were heartwarming.

The white clouds floated by above us. We walked with no words, just the pattering of our feet against the path for sound.

"Angel, how do I know when I find out what I think of God?" I spoke through the quiet.

"I am not sure. Everyone has a different experience." He didn't look at me.

"How do you see Him?" I pressed.

"I will answer that later. We are here."

The next room opened before us. It was very large. We walked in as another city was formed before us. A man stood further ahead, crouching by a small flame.

Chapter 26

The fire was shining across his face. I coughed to get his attention, and he turned to me, smiling slightly.

"James." He turned to face the city once more. "I am the brother of John. We were the 'Sons of Thunder,' a boisterous set. We even asked to be sat one of us on each side of Jesus as He entered into His kingdom. The other disciples were not pleased with us asking to be placed there. That is when Jesus told us the last would become first, and the first would become last.

"From that, I learned you must be a servant. I was a ball of fire, a jealous and angered person. My brother was called the 'beloved' disciple. But were we not alike? Were we not brothers? Eventually, I had to let go of my anger.

"You see that city? I wished heavenly fire on them. It was my Lord who denied my request. The one who was not welcome felt the need to protect the people. Jesus told me to live a life of love, not anger. Once I got to heaven, I played with the children of that city, talked to the men and women. They are such kind people, and I wished death for them."

I shifted my weight to one side, looking at the city in the distance. *He must hurt so much*, I whispered to myself.

"He does. This is a mistake he wishes for you not to make." My angel touched my back softly.

I nodded in understanding, looking back at James. His eyes were on the city still. I did not know what to tell him. Sitting beside him, I thought. I looked at Angel for some kind of help or advice on how to comfort the man, but he just shrugged and looked away. I had to figure it out my own.

As I sat beside him, I felt the heat of the fire, smelled the smoke.

James looked at me with eyes heavy with sadness. "The Lord forgives. He truly loves as He forgives even the worst of sins." He sniffled.

"Will He forgive me for not believing in Him for so long?" I bit my lip as I asked.

"Do you ask for His forgiveness?"

"I think I will soon," I whispered.

He looked at me, surprise and delight in his eyes. He stood, picked me up, and spun me in a circle.

"James, be gentle." My angel playfully punched his arm.

After setting me down, James hit my angel's arm in retaliation. The two wrestled for a moment, both laughing together. My angel fluttered his wings before standing, a laugh deep in his throat.

I watched the two happily. It was as though Angel knew everyone we had met. *He is an angel; he met them here, like he said.* I shrugged as I reasoned with myself.

James came to me, his smile less apparent. He spoke to me. "At the last supper, we were told there was a traitor amongst us. I was afraid. I wondered if it would be me somehow, unable to control myself in a fit of anger or jealousy. The Lord forgives all; be thankful to Him."

The door was beginning to appear.

I smiled to myself, thinking that maybe even I could be loved and forgiven. *No,* the demonic voice called. It was like nails on a chalkboard, like a cloud over my sun. *There is no 'God'. There is no one who wants you.* I closed my eyes in protest.

I felt the door handle in my hand. My eyes shot open. The room had returned to a blinding white. My angel stood beside me, motioning for me to open the door. I turned the handle, hearing it click. The door opened smoothly; not a sound came from it.

Angel led me away slowly, back through the door. We walked side by side. It was peaceful.

The path took a moment to form into its usual landscape. I stopped to smell another small flower. It was beautiful.

"Angel," I began distractedly, "how do you control the emptiness?"

A hardy laugh shook him. "It is not by my will, child, but the Lord's." His eyes melted into a soft kindness.

I nodded as though I believed him, trying not to upset him.

"You need not lie." His eyes retained their warmth.

I stood and took my angel's hand, walking down the path. He held my hand lightly, not applying much pressure.

"Am I near home yet?" I whispered aloud.

"Only a few more child." He gripped my hand slightly harder.

A part of me felt saddened. I enjoyed the attention of heaven, the feeling of being loved. I turned my head, looking to the next room ahead of me. I knew it would be beautiful.

I skipped ahead of Angel, wanting to enjoy the moment fully while I had the chance. I went off the path a short way, walking through the tulips. They were all so beautiful.

I hugged Angel quickly before turning back to the door. Excitement tingled in me like a butterfly trying to escape my heart. Angel gave a short smile, opening the door for me. I walked through it slowly and waited for the next room to begin to form, a smile wide on my face as I waited.

Chapter 27

This room was another field, tulips scattered around it. I smelt the sweet scent of flowers but not tulips. I ignored it and began to look for the person I was to meet inside this room.

A man started towards us from the horizon. "Saint Jude at your service!" he piped cheerfully.

I turned to my angel, hoping for a better introduction.

"Thaddeus." Angel said with a smile.

"Oh." I had not recognized the name at the start.

"It's alright, Lea. Most forget my name," Thaddeus laughed softly. "It's interchangeable between the two."

He sat on the grass, patting on either side of him for my angel and me to join him. We sat beside the man, ready for the new lesson. He played with a few blades of grass before speaking.

"When I was alive, I knew Jesus chose twelve disciples for a reason. We were all different.

Sure, there were some similarities: most of us were fisherman and very outgoing. Most of us wanted to go and preach in the world, excluding certain cities, but Jesus told us to go everywhere.

"He sent us all out to preach, teach, and heal those in need. But nothing we could ever do was as magnificent as His miracles. He let the blind man see, the mute man speak, the lame man walk, and so many more amazing things. He was breathtaking.

"I never understood why He chose twelve *sinners* to walk with Him, but I think I understand now. I am the saint of lost causes. I learned through Jesus that there are no 'lost' causes." He smiled.

"So, what is your lesson?" I asked, hopeful for an answer.

He paused, taking in a deep breath and releasing it slowly before laying back in the grass. "Guess, dear child." He smiled playfully.

"Let me think…" I said. "That there are no lost causes?"

"Ah, she *is* a smart one." He laughed aloud. "But you are missing something."

"What?"

"*In the Lord*, there are no lost causes. You must understand that you need Him just as much as the 'lost causes' need you."

I nodded in understanding. Jesus was needed in my life. I just had to let Him in.

Thaddeus smiled wider. Then, he turned to me, his smile softened with sadness. "The night that some of us have spoken of, the night of Jesus' arrest, I was afraid. I hated knowing that someone would betray Him. I felt lost, knowing that someone would hurt Him. I was afraid. Do not be afraid. Trust in Him and let Him help you."

I looked for the door immediately, knowing it would come as I understood my lesson. It was nowhere in sight.

Thaddeus met my gaze, whispering, "Search for it."

I felt a flame within me, like I had to find my own way home. I stood and walked down a path that led me away from the man.

I walked cautiously. Looking ahead, I noticed a line of trees, so I hurried towards it. As I drew closer, I could tell they were dogwood trees.

I smiled at the blooms on them. The little white flowers with four pink tips had so much meaning to me. I remembered the stories of the trees from my youth. The petals were so soft in my hands. I began to hum a song from my childhood, my favorite hymn.

I saw a cliff towering ahead of me, the door in it. My angel appeared beside me. I grinned at him. He opened the door, letting me walk through. The light on the other side was not harsh but held a warmth to it.

I ran through the tulips, now a darker shade of pink.

My angel laughed at my childish glee. "Hurry now, child. There are not many left to meet," he called.

I stopped as a sudden fear rose in me. *How will my family meet me when I return?* My eagerness to be reunited with them diminished, replaced by dread.

They don't want you. The voices returned. *No one misses you. No one is waiting on the other side.*

My angel must have noticed as he lifted my head towards him. "The Lord will take all problems given to Him."

"How are you always so sure, Angel?" I asked.

"Because *I* gave Him all my troubles. He made me feel whole again. Trust Him, Lea."

I did not believe him, mainly because it seemed impossible for this problem to be taken away.

My angel let out a heavy sigh.

It left an uncomfortable chill in me. I looked forward; the next room loomed before us.

He walked beside me, deep in thought. The quiet fell

over us. I did not meet his eyes as we passed through the door.

He did smile down at me, though, however faintly. It was nice to see his smile again.

Chapter 28

The room was wide; a city was far in the distance. The next man I was to meet was sitting on a rock beside me.

"Are you afraid of death?" He stared at the city.

"I am already dead," I retorted with a snort.

"No, child. You are not." My angel spoke in the man's place. "Like I have told you, we are just walking right outside the gates of heaven. You are still very much alive, just in a coma on Earth."

"What? You mean I'm still alive?" I gasped.

My stomach twisted some. I knew my family was worried about me. I knew they were probably at my bedside, waiting for me to wake up. Fear twinged inside me. How would they greet me? Would they even still love me? Angel touched my shoulder to try and comfort me.

"I did not fear death when I was with my Lord." The man continued as though he had not heard Angel and me. "I wished to die with Him, for Him. Yet I did not." I saw a single tear glide down his cheek. "I am only known for my doubt. One wrong thing has become my legacy."

"Thomas?" I spun to see my angel.

He bowed his head in answer.

"Mary and Martha's brother was dying, and they sent for Jesus. We were all scared. Yet I stood and called for action, saying to the others that we should go and die with Him. Does that sound like a coward? The world did not like the God Jesus spoke of, a Father of love and kindness.

"The religious leaders of the day had my Savior killed. Tensions were high. The others were hiding in the upper room. Mary told them of seeing the Lord, and they doubted her. *They* doubted, every single one of them.

"They saw Jesus the first time He came to them. Then, they believed. Yet when I returned and doubted what they said, telling them I would only believe if I could touch his wounds, *I* became the one famous for doubting. Why am I only remembered for a weakness in my faith?" he cried out.

Thomas was slumped over on the rock he sat on. I rubbed his back, not sure of what to say. He turned his sad face to me.

"My lesson is to be brave and to never doubt the Lord." A sigh escaped his lips. "Do not become like me. Believe if the Lord so wants you to."

I felt a stab in my heart. I was bewildered by seeing one of the great saints like this, completely distraught.

"Thomas, are you alright?" The words came from my mouth without hesitation.

He smiled to me. "It is well with my soul as my Lord is with me."

I saw the faint outline of the man I kept seeing beside him, though I could not see His face through the light.

"It can't be," I whispered aloud, blinking roughly to try and clear my eyes.

"You see him, no?" Thomas rose to stand beside me.

"I have been…" My words came like an unseen wind.

He laughed. "She sees you, good Lord!" He yowled toward the sky with joy. I could not help but giggle as he skipped around me, dancing.

"Thomas, how can you be so gleeful when you have just cried?" My angel laughed with his friend.

"Because the good Lord is in her; He stays with her," he replied happily.

I smiled at the two. It was wonderful to see them smile together like old friends, though I was not sure why.

"That night, the night of the last supper," Thomas turned to me quickly, "I believed in Him more than anything else. Now, go and believe in Him also."

The door had appeared moments ago, yet I felt no need to rush to the next room.

My angel walked towards the door, though. "Are we ready to go?" He smiled down to me.

I nodded slightly. "Goodbye, Thomas." I waved to him.

"Let it be well with your soul." His words carried confidence within them.

My angel opened the door letting me walk through. I began down the path once more. I looked at the tulips, now a deep red. A small, pale butterfly flapped past my nose.

"Angel, look! Isn't he beautiful?" I turned to where I thought my angel was, but he was not there.

"Angel?" I called out, a sudden fear filtering through me.

I looked around desperately for him. I could not see him anywhere, though. My heart started beating faster. It felt like it was not moving at all. My head started to hurt as fear set in. I did not want to be alone. I wanted my angel with me. I continued to search for him, going off the path and into the tulip field further and further.

"Angel, please! I need you!" I screamed.

I shivered as the red tulips were pushed in the wind towards the path. As I got back onto the path, having found no sign of Angel, the tulips waved toward the next room. I stared at them, brilliantly red in the bright sun.

I turned back toward the next room. *He must be in there*, I reasoned with myself. I ran to it, hating being alone. I felt tears flow from my eyes.

"Angel! Where are you?" I choked on my words and the cool air.

I ran into the room as fast as I could. I could not breath. It felt like water was filling my lungs. I kept running, not fully seeing where I was going as the tears blurred my vision.

The white box blurred out but came closer like it had every time before as the room began to mold into another landscape. There was no one. I was alone. I hated being alone.

Chapter 29

The sun was casting deep reds and oranges across the pale sky. A single tree sat on a small, rocky hill a short distance ahead of me. I walked down the thin, red dirt path to it. The tree was dark, twisted with age and weather. I ran my hand across the course bark; it was as rough as it looked.

Soft footsteps sounded dully behind me. I turned to see the owner, only to find my angel without his wings and dressed in dirty brown clothes.

"Dear child…" His smile was sad but still held a warmth to it. He let out a heavy sigh, shaking his head as though in protest. I felt my heart sink as he spoke. "My name is Judas Iscariot, betrayer of the Lord."

His words rang in my ears, sending tremors down my spine. "That can't be," I breathed out. "Stop lying, Angel. It isn't funny."

His eyes glistened with pain. "But it is true. I am the hated one," he whimpered.

"Angel, seriously. Stop joking. If you're really Judas, why are you here? Why are you *my* angel?" I began crying.

"I'm sorry, Lea. I had to hide my identity from you. I knew you would not trust me if I told you who I am."

"You lied to me! How could you?" I snapped.

"I am sorry. I had to," he cried.

"How are you here?" I stared at him. His eyes looked aged with agony.

"Let me explain, dear child. I was not from Galilee; I was from Judea. I was an outcast from the start," he began. "While the other disciples were heavenly-minded, I was worldly-minded. I was the treasurer for us. I held the money to feed us, to pay temple taxes, to give to the poor, to use for whatever was needed. I once criticized Mary for using expensive perfume to wash Jesus' feet. Jesus often spoke of greed and money, and I am sure it was because of me. Yet, I ignored it.

"Everyone wanted Jesus to become king and drive out the Romans. I felt like the only way to do that was through a greater miracle than any He had already done.

"Then, that night, the night of the last supper we had together, He spoke of a traitor. And the morsel He fed me? That small bite of bread tasted like heaven, like wheat blown by sweet smelling air, like a warm blessing. Then, the wine, like poison, entered me, and in that moment, my heart turned to stone, letting evil fill me.

"He washed my feet as though to give me another chance, yet I still left to sell my Savior. I was given thirty pieces of silver, a slave's price in my time, for someone who loved me. Thirty pieces of silver blood money in exchange for the blood of the world's Lamb.

"I gathered the men and led them to the garden, a garden we had been to many times. The men told Jesus they were looking for Jesus of Nazareth. They fell back as He spoke. I walked past the men, kissing Him on the cheek. A kiss of all things, a sign of love and respect, sold the man who spoke of nothing but love. How foolish.

"Jesus stared into my eyes. I saw my life in them, all my sins and regrets. Then they changed back to his magnificent ones, softened with sorrow.

"Peter tried to protect Him, but Jesus stopped him. As they took Him away, I knew what I had done.

"I ran to the chief priest, throwing the money at his feet, begging to get my Lord back. Yet he refused. I left and did the only thing I could think to do." His words were broken with sorrow caught in his throat.

"But how did you get here, in heaven of all places? You don't deserve to be here." I felt tears in my eyes.

"When I made it to Heaven, Jesus met me there with open arms. He told me what had happened. I felt free and loved in that moment."

Tears stained the red dirt beneath Judas, my angel. His head hung down in shame.

I tried to think of what to say. But no words came. I stared at him in silence for what felt like forever. I hated the silence.

A soft hand touched my shoulder, and white cloth began to surround me. I did not look back in fear that the person would be gone.

"I am here with you, my child," a booming voice, like thunder, announced.

I should have been afraid, but I was not. It was like love had touched me for the first time. I felt at peace. All felt right. I knew Jesus was there.

The hand was gone, and I looked at Angel. I walked to him, taking his hand. "Angel, are there sinners in heaven?" I asked again through a voice that was breaking like glass, faking a smile.

"Everyone is a sinner. But through Jesus, anyone can get into heaven. Here I am, the sinner of sinners, in beautiful heaven. Everyone you have met here was a sinner, and through the forgiveness of God, they made it to heaven, too," he answered finally.

"Will I be able to get into heaven?" I whispered.

"Once you let Him back into your life, anything is possible." He nodded.

I looked at the tree, shivering. Turning back to Angel, I smiled shakily, drying my tears. "What's next?" I asked, playfully tapping his arm.

"You go home." He smiled sadly.

The door appeared behind him. I opened it and waited for him to go through. He shook his head, his eyes sad and knowing.

"I can't come with you this time. I'll watch over you, but this may be the last time we see each other for a while." Tears still glistened in his eyes as he looked at me.

"Goodbye, Angel. Take care of everyone for me." I waved at him sadly.

I walked through the door and into the red tulip field. The world spread out before me for miles. It was a quiet walk to the next door. Only the soft hum of the world and the sweet chirps of bird song could be heard. I listened; the voices in my head were unusually silent. I was at peace.

I finally came up to the door. I looked back, staring at the other door far in the distance. I shook my head and walked through the one in front of me.

Chapter 30

I opened my eyes slowly. The room was dark. I looked out the window to see the city. The lights were flickering like stars at night. I looked to my side, seeing my father asleep beside me in a chair. His hand was in mine. I squeezed it gently.

"Dad," I croaked out. My throat was sore.

He stretched awake, looking around for whomever had woken him. He gasped as I smiled at him. He pulled me close, crying as he spoke.

"Lea, I thought I'd lost you! I don't know what I would do without you," he sobbed. He woke my sister and pulled her close to me. I remember how they were crying like they were afraid of losing me. That made me realize I have a place where I belong.

They told me I had been in a coma for a while, though I already knew that. I pretended not to as I was not ready to share what I had experienced. I was afraid of not being believed. I was

not sure if I completely believed
it.

I stayed in the hospital for
a few weeks as I was regaining
strength. As soon as I was
cleared, the doctors admitted me
into a psychiatric hospital.

It was quiet there. The
nurses were always sweet and
calm. The hospital pastor spoke
with me, to see if I had accepted
Jesus into my life. He was the first
one I talked about my journey to.
He believed me. He went so far
as to help foster my faith and help
me find a way to share what I
experienced.

I spent the weeks in the psychiatric hospital learning to pray again. Throughout my time there, I even saw Angel a few times. I wanted to make it my mission to help others the way I needed help.

Once I was discharged, I spent a while doing monthly therapy until I felt as though I had done some healing and was comfortable enough to move on. I never heard the voices again; a mix of medication and prayers took them away. I was a lucky one. My recovery was quick and easy.

I never relapsed into "the hole." By some miracle, I had been pulled out. I worked and prayed hard to never return. My family even agreed to go to a local church with me every few Sundays. I fell back in love with my religion.

I remember one Sunday; a new person came into our church. His name was Elijah. He had this smile that melted my heart. He walked into a pew on his way to introduce himself to me. It reminded me of how my parents met.

After a few years, Elijah and I got married. He confessed

to having a dream the day before we met, in which he saw a small red-headed boy. Elijah told me the boy looked like me. I knew in an instant this man was Jeremiah's father.

Elijah supported me in my dreams of helping others. So much so he helped me start "Hearing Angels". Hearing Angels was a home for anyone who needed it. We were mainly used as a psychiatric outpatient organization, but we had others come to us for help.

Hearing Angels became a home for my family. Jeremiah even roamed the halls with his "imaginary friend" Angel. I knew who it was. I knew my angel would protect my family.

We all showed what the world had to offer and what the Lord wanted to give to them instead. The people we saved grew to share our message.

I would not change my life for anything. It was rough sometimes; some of our friends in need chose not to listen and left without faith. Those cases always saddened me. However, I knew love always won, so I gave them my love regardless.

I tried to teach others every lesson I had learned from

the angels I had met. Many people thought I was lying about my time there. Others believed and knew my truth. I tried to help everyone understand His great love.

Everything I experienced in my life was a blessing, even if I did not know it or feel like it was at the time. Sometimes, the bad comes before the good. I knew what my purpose was, though I could not say many were lucky enough to know.

I learned not to run from God but to go where He sent me. Every second of my life was worth living. A lot of my questions were answered once I returned to Earth, even the ones the angels had already answered for me. I was just a skeptical person who chose to learn for herself.

I finally know my answer. I have experienced it, and now I believe it.

Are there sinners in heaven?

Through God, there are.